Storms of Death

Storms of Death

Nathan Jay

JNJ Publishing LLC

CONTENTS

CONTENTS

1

Whispers of Evil

Asura held her wrinkled hand over Claire's face as she lay sleeping on the ground. Suddenly, a blue flame exploded from her index finger and engulfed her hand. Smiling, the old woman moved it closer to Claire's face.

"It's what you deserve," the witch whispered.

The color on Claire's face began to change, fading and then becoming white like ash. Her skin started sizzling until, finally, the tissue melted away to reveal the red muscle and cartilage around her jawbone.

Seeing the damage to Claire pleased Asura, and she smiled. But soon, her smile disappeared. She gnashed her teeth and grimaced from the pain radiating through her hand. Although the fire burned Claire's face, using the dark magic made Asura's fingers freeze. Her arm started cracking as the numbing cold crawled slowly up her wrist until her whole arm became a block of ice.

"Your seed has hurt my master," whispered Asura, the blue flame lighting her wicked eyes.

Although her frozen arm was heavy, Asura continued holding the flame over Claire's face. Soon, the fire caused Claire's gumline to recede, exposing the root of her teeth. Asura trembled in joy as the flame of her dark magic degraded Claire's teeth; the nerves underneath became plump with puss until they burst, shooting thick yellow fluid onto

Asura's face. Finally, holes appeared in the enamel of her teeth, and Claire started moaning.

"Arlo, where are you?" moaned Claire. "It hurts."

Asura's eyes were wide with excitement as she watched the woman's half-melted face twitch. Seeing Claire's suffering excited Asura so much that she ignored the pain coming from her frozen arm. She didn't notice the rustling behind her until it was too late; John stood over Asura and saw what she was doing.

"What are you doing?" asked John.

Startled, Asura pulled her hand back, and Claire's jaw immediately returned to normal.

"Master! I thought you were sleeping," responded Asura. "Do you need something?"

John sighed and sat beside the old woman on the ground.

"Claire took care of me in my younger years. Do not harm her."

Annoyed, Asura grumbled and covered her frozen arm. She aimed her finger at the wood pile before them and ignited the campfire.

"Excuse me, Lord. I'm angry."

John shook his head and rose from the ground. He walked to the cave entrance and looked into the dark, rainy forest. Seconds later, Asura walked over and stood behind him.

"We will need to contact Lord Balam soon," said John.

Asura caressed John's arm.

"Are you afraid?"

"I am."

"But it wasn't your fault. The Angels interfered."

"Explanations do nothing to change what has happened."

"Do you think Lord Balam knows?"

John turned to face Asura.

"She knows."

"Why hasn't she come for you?"

"She's probably watching to see if I'll betray her. But I will not evade responsibility. At sunrise, I'll initiate contact."

"How? This cave won't accommodate Lord Balam's arrival. There's no one to kill, and we don't have human intestines to initiate contact."

"Yes. I know," said John.

"We could kill Arlo's mother," said Asura, nodding toward Claire.

"No, Asura. I won't do that."

Asura stared at John in silence. Finally, she spoke.

"Use me."

John stared at Asura in disbelief.

"Are you sure? The process is painful."

"I'll use my powers to protect myself."

"There is no protection from hell."

"I understand. But what other choice do we have?"

"You don't need to do this, Asura. I don't want to risk your life."

Asura smiled and touched John's face.

"I made a promise to be by your side forever. I will not abandon my master when he's vulnerable. Your pain is my pain."

John looked into the wet forest while Asura turned and frowned at Claire as she lay sleeping by the fire.

"What about her?"

"If Arlo attacks, we'll use her as insurance. But if Arlo doesn't come for us, you can release her into the forest when the time is right."

"Release her? But her son just destroyed our plans!"

"Look at me, Asura. You will not harm her. Is that understood? Her son destroyed our plans, not Mrs. Ortega. Until she does something to interfere directly, we will exercise restraint."

Asura sighed and reluctantly accepted John's words.

"Where will you contact Lord Balam?"

John pointed into the forest.

"There in the clearing. Come with me."

Asura grabbed John's arm and pulled him back.

"Wait. There's something you should know."

"What is it?"

"Betrayal."

John turned to face Asura.

"Betrayal? What do you mean?"

"We forced the Witches of Blood Mountain to fortify the Huturo using their sorcery."

"They did. So?"

Asura stepped into the rain and held up her hand.

"I didn't realize it until we ran from the hospital, but the water composition changed."

John seemed confused, so Asura scooped some water from a puddle and poured it into his hand.

"What's wrong with this water?"

John dipped his finger in the fluid.

"It's thick, almost like snot. And it's heavy."

"Right. There's another spell inside the water, hidden beneath the original spell we had the witches cast for us. That's the reason the raindrops feel thick and heavy. "

"The witches cast another spell? But why?"

"For whatever reason, the Witches of Blood Mountain decided to join Arlo. The attack at the hospital wasn't a small group of zombies; it was only the beginning. I can feel the numbers of the undead multiplying, and the witches gave Arlo the power to control them all."

"This doesn't make sense. Clairvoyants are powerful, so why would they follow a dead teenager?"

"Maybe the witches see Hell's invasion as threatening to all creatures. Those good-for-nothing bitches were always arrogant. Too bad they weren't smart enough to avoid the Spell of Xavier – the only conjuration Heaven explicitly forbids."

"The Spell of Xavier? What is that?"

"It's the second spell the Witches hid under the first. It gives Arlo the power to control the undead."

"And Heaven forbids this?"

"Absolutely. The Spell of Xavier is the only conjuration universally banned in all ancient and modern sorcery texts."

"What happens if someone breaks the rule?"

"They're removed from the Scrolls of Life."

"What's that?"

"The Scrolls of Life is where God writes the actual name of every creature before they're born, and it guarantees eternal life to every soul after the accounting of their sins. I only know of one way to have your name removed from the scrolls – by using the Spell of Xavier."

John thought about his desire to take his place at Balam's side in Hell. After thinking for a moment, he spoke.

"Turning to Hell doesn't guarantee removal?"

"No, because you always have a shot at redemption. But using the Spell of Xavier is different; you're turning resting souls into evil weapons. These are people whose lives have ended and are awaiting their passage - only God has the power to wake them for judgment. By interrupting their sleep, you're essentially stealing from God and using the spirits for evil."

"What happens when Heaven decides to remove someone?"

"When Heaven removes a soul from the Scrolls of Life, they wipe away your existence—complete and total obliteration. But Heaven doesn't stop there. They also destroy the person's bloodline. Their mother, father, grandparents, and cousins - the entire family is gone forever. There's no Heaven or Hell for any of them - it'll be like they were never born."

"If the Witches of Blood Mountain know the penalty for using the Spell of Xavier, why would they risk it?"

Asura scooped another handful of muddy water from the ground and ran her finger through it.

"Every witch leaves a detectable signature in their spells, but I do not detect the signatures of the Witches of Blood Mountain in this water."

"Which means they hid their identities."

"That's my guess. If Heaven found out the witches were responsible, the Angels would be combing the hills of Blood Mountain. But they're not there. They're here in the Black Forest."

John was silent for a moment.

"It's Arlo! The Witches of Blood Mountain erased any trace of their responsibility but left Arlo's identity intact. The Angels aren't here for the witches; they're here to kill Arlo!"

John ran towards the clearing with Asura following closely behind.

"Hurry! We have to initiate contact with Lord Balam. We might be able to use this situation to our advantage."

As John and Asura ran into the forest, neither realized Claire was awake and had been listening to their conversation. After they were out of sight, Claire crept out of the cave and ran in the opposite direction.

2

Infiltration

"Wait," whispered Isadora inside her mind.

She grabbed Arlo's arm, and they stopped moving through the forest.

"What is it?" asked Arlo.

"Do you see that over there?" replied Isadora, pointing to a clump of bushes beyond the building.

The plants were trembling as though something was shaking them. Suddenly, weird violet bulbs sprouted from the plant, growing large until they finally fell to the ground. A thick, dark mist engulfed the plant when the strange fruit touched the soil. Suddenly, the black roots of the plants exploded out of the earth, crawled across the forest floor, and wrapped themselves around several trees, squeezing until a thick red liquid dripped from the bark.

"That's the same plant from the dead Huturo," said Arlo.

"Yeah," replied Isadora. *"It's spreading."*

Arlo looked around nervously.

"If the plant is here, that means...."

"The vampires!"

Isadora looked up in the sky and saw an enormous bird with eyes of fire descend and land on the rooftop of the small building. After a few seconds, the bird's eyes returned to normal, and it flew away.

"Forneus is inside the building. We've got to warn him."

The two zombies stumbled through the forest toward the shack. Before they reached the building, they heard Forneus's screams echoing inside their heads.

"AHHHHH! GET OUT OF HERE!" he bellowed.

Arlo and Isadora stood before the building, waiting for Forneus to emerge. When he didn't, they began to panic.

"Are we going in?" asked Isadora.

"We just can't let him battle that thing alone. We have to do something!" replied Arlo.

Just as they were about to enter, a giant white blur flew past them and crashed into a tree. They turned and saw a pale, naked woman with long gray hair lying on the ground. Slowly, the woman stood and turned to face the teenagers – there were tiny mouths all over her body, and instead of eyes, there were two mouths filled with teeth in her eye sockets.

"Holy shit!" said Arlo.

"A vampire!" replied Isadora.

Arlo grabbed Isadora's arm and ducked behind a nearby bush. The sound of the rustling leaves made the vampire turn in their direction. The creature tilted its head, listening while thick yellow saliva began pouring from the mouths on her body. Soon, another rustling came, and the vampire jerked her head from side to side, trying to pinpoint the location of the sound. Finally, the source of the sound revealed itself: a squirrel scattering on the trunk of a nearby tree. Before the creature took another step, the vampire grabbed it, pressed the struggling creature to her forearm, and began draining the animal of all its bodily fluids. Arlo and Isadora watched silently as the squirrel's body melted away like butter until its ashes fell to the ground.

Satisfied there was nothing more of its victim to consume, the vampire stood and tilted its head, searching for more food. There was a rustling of leaves to her right, and she turned to listen, the mouths on her body leaking more of the thick, putrid fluid. Suddenly, two more vampires emerged from the woods, a muscular man and a teenage boy. Both were naked, with hundreds of sucking mouths all over their bodies.

The sight of the vampires frightened Isadora.

"Arlo!" she said nervously inside her mind. *"Call the zombies!"*

Arlo remembered the army of zombies under his control in the forest behind them. It would be easy to summon the undead to defend Forneus, but Arlo hesitated. Something about what he was witnessing made him nervous. Instead of calling for reinforcements, he eyed the vampires silently, looking for a sign of weakness.

"Arlo!" said Isadora again. *"Hurry up! You've got to do something!"*

"Not yet," replied Arlo.

"But we're outnumbered."

"Killing the Huturo created the vampires. But what happens when we kill the vampires? It could be something much worse. Try to relax."

Arlo concentrated and sent mental commands to the hundreds of zombies in the forest.

"Climb the trees and hide."

Suddenly, the tops of the trees around them began swaying, making leaves rain down on Arlo and Isadora. The vampires on the ground seemed confused, and they frantically turned around, looking up at the trees. Their bodies began emitting loud puckering noises, and their skin began to shine from the fluid pouring from the mouths on their bodies. When they could not find any victims within their reach, they ran to the first vampire and paused before falling to their knees to sniff the remains of the dead squirrel. After realizing they couldn't eat the squirrel, the monsters raised their heads and shrieked in frustration before all three sprinted into the forest in search of more victims.

When the vampires were gone, Forneus emerged from the building, clutching his arm. He spotted Arlo and Isadora hiding in the bushes and stumbled over to them, his enormous skeleton body shaking uncontrollably.

"Forneus, are you okay?" asked Isadora.

"*Argggggh,*" groaned Forneus while holding up his left arm to reveal a missing hand. "*I'll be okay in a minute.*"

Arlo and Isadora watched as the snakes inside the glass casing on Forneus's chest began glowing and thrashing around. Soon, Forneus's bones in his missing hand regenerated along with strings of veins and tissue that spread across the bones, wrapping around his fingers. After a few seconds, a human hand made of flesh was on the skeleton's wrist.

"*Arggggh,*" Forneus groaned again.

Suddenly, the hand turned black, and all the skin fell off, leaving only a skeletal hand. Forneus opened and closed his fist and sighed in relief.

"*We must leave. This place is no longer safe,*" said Forneus.

"*Where will we go?*" asked Arlo.

Forneus walked to the pile of dust that was once the squirrel and looked around suspiciously before kneeling to inspect the remains.

"*What is it, Forneus?*" asked Arlo.

Forneus ripped a branch off the nearest tree and dipped it into the ashes. As soon as he did, the wood burst into a black flame. Forneus dropped the tree branch and moved away from the fire.

"*What kind of devilment is this?*" he asked.

Forneus watched the burning black flame until it went out. He turned around and looked into the forest.

"*Killing these things always seems to bring something worse.*"

"*That's why I told the undead to hide in the trees. I remembered how the Huturo multiplied when they died and thought it best to be careful.*"

Arlo walked to the building and peered inside.

"*How did that thing get into the building?*"

"*We were careless. I didn't put the stone in place before we left; the creature must've smelled decay on the pile of bones we left inside. I would be dead if more than one of those creatures were inside the building.*"

"*How many do you think are out there?*"

"*It's hard to say. I'm sure others have figured out how to kill the Huturo, so there could be hundreds – thousands.*"

"*Jeez.*"

Forneus walked to a stone on the side of the entrance and sat down. The glowing worms inside his skull began twisting wildly, and Forneus grabbed his head in agony.

"This whole situation is disturbing," said Forneus.

"What's bothering you, Forneus?" asked Arlo.

The giant skeleton opened his bony mouth and sighed.

"Reason. That's what's bothering me."

"Reason?"

"Why is Hell attacking, and why now?"

"That's easy," piped Isadora. *"Good versus Evil, right?"*

Forneus shook his head in disagreement.

"Heaven's power over Hell is unquestionable. While the kingdom of Heaven rarely displays such might, it's there, and Hell knows it. So what does Hell do to avoid the wrath of God? They lie and cheat, convincing people to surrender their souls willfully."

"Plausible deniability," said Isadora.

"What?" asked Arlo. *"What's that?"*

"Hell is guilty but doesn't want the perception of guilt. That way, if Heaven confronts them, they can say, 'We didn't take a soul; they gave it to us.'"

"Yeah? And?" asked Arlo.

"Look at everything that's happening. Monsters that never die plant life from other worlds, the demons.... These things are invasive, disrespectful, and aggressive. It almost feels like Hell is trying to piss Heaven off."

"You're right," agreed Arlo. *"The whole thing seems pretty blatant when you think about it."*

The worms inside Forneus's skull lit up again.

"It's obvious that Hell isn't afraid of Heaven anymore, and we need to figure out why. It's only a matter of time before Heaven confronts them for their transgressions. And when that happens...."

Arlo and Isadora looked at each other.

"The end of the world," whispered Arlo.

"What are we going to do?" asked Isadora.

"We've got to move to higher ground. There's one place I'm pretty sure the vampires haven't reached: Hollow Spirit Mountain."

"Hollow Spirit Mountain? That sounds like the perfect place for the undead."

Forneus looked at Isadora with his blazing eyes.

"Believe me. You won't like this place. It's void of all life, only rocks and sand."

"How will we get food?"

"I'll use the birds to hunt for us from the skies. It'll be clumsy, but none of us will be at risk."

Isadora stumbled over to Forneus and stood before him.

"Is this Armageddon, Forneus?"

Although Isadora was speaking inside her mind, Arlo could hear the unmistakable fear in her voice.

"I don't know," replied Forneus.

The skeleton's response seemed to agitate Isadora, and she began peppering Forneus with questions.

"It can't be the end. What about all the innocent people? What about our families? What about...."

Forneus didn't let her finish.

"Don't do this to yourself. If this is Armageddon, we can do nothing to stop it. The opportunity to save your family is gone. Just as Arlo could not help his mother, your family will also perish."

Forneus walked to the entrance of the building.

"Prepare yourselves. We're leaving in a few minutes."

Arlo walked behind the skeleton.

"Hey, Forneus. What do we do about all the zombies out there? There's no way we can take all of them with us."

"These zombies are only a small portion of the numerous zombies under your control."

"But these few here are loud and clumsy."

"Maybe, but that's a good thing. Use this small army to sharpen your abilities. The power to control them belongs only to you. But with each *passing day, the army of zombies grows larger. Soon you'll be in control of millions of the undead."*

Arlo's mouth fell open.

"Millions?"

"You need to practice controlling them, or you'll be overwhelmed. When the zombies outnumber the Huturo, Hell will send reinforcements - creatures far worse than anything you can imagine."

"And how will we fight then?"

The question annoyed Forneus, and he turned away from Arlo.

"Stop behaving like a spineless coward and do as I say! Your attention should be on the battle before you, not the future battle!"

"But you said...."

Forneus punched the large stone at the entrance.

"This is the only chance I have!"

The worms inside Forneus's skull began shrieking, and the gigantic skeleton walked inside the building, leaving the teens alone.

Isadora walked to Arlo's side and stared at the building until Forneus's glowing eyes disappeared inside.

"I hate when he gets like this."

"What do you mean?"

"He has these spells. One moment, he's being nice to us and sending us to the Priming Fields to rejuvenate our souls, and then a few days later, he's coming at us with this crap."

"I'm confused."

"You don't see it? This asshole behavior is part of his selfishness."

"How?"

"He's not telling you the whole truth."

"And what's that?"

"He's using you to get back to his wife."

"I know. So?"

"That doesn't frighten you?"

"What's the worst that can happen to me? Death? I'd welcome that, wouldn't you?"

Air escaped the hole in Isadora's rotting face as she tried to sigh and pressed her decomposing body against Arlo's.

"With Hell, it's never about just dying. They will do horrible things to you, or worse – they'll enslave your soul."

Arlo looked into Isadora's decomposing face and tried to smile.

"Nobody lives forever."

3

The Visitors

It was dark and raining heavily when Arlo and Isadora started walking toward the city. As the storm drenched them, the two looked up in the dark sky frequently; Forneus was flying overhead in the body of an enormous red owl, the light from his fiery eyes darting in and out of the dark clouds, casting intermittent beams of light on the forest to show them the way.

Arlo and Isadora held hands as they moved through the forest; everything was so dark they could barely see where they were going. Occasionally, Forneus would fly low in a circle, alerting the teenagers of monsters in their path, and they would need to change course. Meanwhile, Arlo would send the command in his mind, and the forest would tremble as the hundreds of zombies climbed the trees or changed course to follow Arlo and Isadora.

Eating was also necessary, and Forneus would randomly drop squirrels and small rodents from the skies that he collected in his bird form. Arlo and Isadora would grab the tiny creatures and suck their brains out before tossing their little corpses aside to continue their journey. Finding food for the other zombies proved to be the biggest challenge. Arlo would ask Forneus to fly low over the forest to see if any creatures were around. If there were none, Arlo would instruct the zombies to run behind them in search of animals to kill. After waiting an hour, he would command the undead to return to their original positions.

"This isn't so bad," whispered Isadora.

Arlo didn't respond to her comment. He spotted a squirrel on a tree trunk, grabbed it, and ripped the animal's head off, sucking out its brains in one motion. After emptying the animal's skull, Arlo tossed it aside and stuck his fingers into its guts, hooking it around his finger and pulling it out until it dangled from the corpse. Arlo threw back his head, and like spaghetti, he sucked on the creature's insides until its entrails fell into his mouth.

"Do you ever think about the Priming Fields?" asked Isadora, grabbing another nearby squirrel from the tree.

Arlo silently licked the blood from his fingers.

Isadora made quick work of the animal by using her two thumbs to open the creature's belly, grabbing its organs, and shoving them into her mouth. She chewed and swallowed the animal's organs, saving its brain for last, which she promptly sucked out.

"It was so nice to see ourselves as we used to be," Isadora continued. *"I hope we get to revisit one day."*

"Uh-huh."

Arlo wasn't paying attention - he was too busy searching the trees for other animals to eat.

Isadora stopped walking and pulled Arlo's arm.

"What's up with you?"

"Nothing."

"I know this whole situation is shit, but do you have to be so drab?"

"It's nothing, okay? I'm just thinking about what we have to do."

Isadora sighed, and the two continued walking.

Arlo didn't know how to tell Isadora why he only provided one-word responses. The effects of the decomposition of his body weighed on him like a car on a flat tire; the air around him was far too thin, and his lungs didn't work. And now a red tinge was covering the world he saw, making everything appear drenched in blood.

Finally, Isadora noticed Arlo's eyes shifting erratically, and she stopped walking.

"Arlo, are you okay?"

"I'm fine."

"You're changing, aren't you? We all have to go through the process."

"I said I'm fine, Isadora."

Isadora grabbed Arlo's shoulders and pulled him close.

"Yep, I knew it. Your eyes are completely white now."

Arlo pushed Isadora's hands away.

"I said I'm fine!"

But Arlo wasn't okay. In addition to his body's deterioration, Arlo couldn't stop thinking of eating brains – human brains. Although Arlo was walking through the stormy forest with Isadora at his side, his mind was in the hunter's cabin, the place of his first kill. He replayed the murder of the old man continuously, relishing in the metallic taste of his blood and the victim's trembling body as Arlo lay on his victim, sucking the life out of his body through the opening in his skull. Before, Arlo had been horrified by the act, but now he longed to hear the man's last gasps, the pungent odor of old cigarettes and shit, as the man's bowels released everything inside him as Arlo ate his brains. Arlo wanted that feeling so much now. He longed for it as a dry thirst longed for cool water. Arlo needed, no, wanted to kill again. He had to.

Finally, Arlo and Isadora arrived at a clearing in the forest. Arlo looked up in the rainy sky and saw Forneus flying low in a circle over the area.

"I think he wants us to stop here," Arlo told Isadora.

Arlo removed the bag he'd been carrying over his shoulder and poured the contents on the ground; they were Forneus's abnormally large bones, and he needed them close whenever he wanted to return to his original form. He looked up in the rain and saw something strange: pink petals falling from the sky. Arlo grabbed one of the petals from his hair and stared at it –a Cherry Blossom petal.

"What's that?" asked Isadora.

"A Cherry Blossom," replied Arlo.

Isadora grabbed one of the petals from a puddle on the grass.

"Cherry Blossoms? How? There aren't any Cherry Blossom trees in this forest."

Arlo called out to Forneus in his mind.

"Forneus! Can you hear me?"

"Yes, I can hear you. I'm coming down."

"What are all these petals?"

"What do you mean?"

"Cherry Blossom petals are falling from the sky. Can't you see them?"

Forneus paused.

"We have visitors. Don't try to run, or they'll...."

Forneus didn't get a chance to finish his sentence. As the bird descended, everything suddenly froze; its wings stopped flapping, and the creature remained suspended in the air while the raindrops around it dangled, shimmering like tiny ice crystals. A powerful gust of wind from above pushed down on Isadora and Arlo, knocking them to the ground and covering them in Cherry Blossom petals. Arlo tried to get up, but the wind continued blowing, plastering his arms and legs to the forest floor, making it impossible for him to rise.

"I can't move!" Arlo yelled.

"Me either! What's happening?" asked Isadora, her rotting body stuck in a mud puddle.

Arlo looked up at Forneus; the bird remained motionless beneath the black clouds. Suddenly, a long bolt of lightning struck the bird.

"Ahhhhhhh!" screamed Forneus, the owl's shriek and his voice combining in an agonizing cry of pain.

Another bolt of lightning shot out of a nearby cloud and struck the bird, illuminating all the bones in the creature's body like an X-ray. Suddenly, a white light opened beneath the birth, and a ghostly figure tumbled slowly, drifting down to the earth like a leaf on a breeze.

Arlo watched in silence as the man falling from the sky drew closer, his ghostly body struggling to hold its form like an image on a snowy tv.

It was the first time Arlo saw Forneus in his human form, and he didn't look anything like the monster Arlo had become accustomed to seeing. Forneus was much taller than an average human, with muscles pushing out from all over his body like a bodybuilder. He had long black hair and angry brown eyes. His long arms and hands told Arlo that Forneus had been a manual laborer in his previous life, possibly a farm hand or a steelworker.

"That's Forneus?" asked Isadora.

"Yeah, I think so," replied Arlo.

As Forneus drifted slowly toward the ground, he was cursing and sneering, but nothing came out of his mouth. His brown eyes, now empty of flames, searched the forest for his captors as he punched the air angrily, trying to free himself. Finally, he stopped falling and remained suspended high in the air.

The trees on the other side of the clearing began shaking.

"Arlo," whispered Isadora inside Arlo's head. *"I'm scared."*

Suddenly, the trees parted, and a tall figure draped in a white robe emerged from the darkness. Arlo tried to move, but his body failed him.

"Oh no," whispered Isadora. *"Is that one of Hell's new creatures?"*

Arlo could tell the being was human and watched silently as the figure moved closer, its long blonde hair concealing its identity. As the figure walked across the Cherry Blossom petals, they began to glow, floating around the figure as if magnetized by the figure's presence.

Suddenly, the stranger stopped walking. Without lifting a finger, the person's long hair moved away from his face, revealing a handsome man with deep bronze-colored skin that shimmered like glitter. The man stopped walking toward Arlo and stood staring at him from the middle of the field. Arlo stared back uncomfortably, not knowing if he should try to speak with his monster-like voice or attempt a conversation as he talked to Isadora.

Suddenly, Arlo heard a fluttering sound, and two enormous multi-colored wings spread out from the man's back. The angel turned away from Arlo and looked up at the sky.

"Forneus," called the angel.

Forneus continued struggling and cursing at the angel, but nothing came out of his mouth.

"My name is Jamison," he said, bowing slightly. "This is my sister, Malaika."

Jamison pointed in Isadora's and Arlo's direction.

There was a burst of light, and warm air rushed over Arlo and Isadora. Suddenly, a glass silhouette appeared above the teenagers. Slowly, the glass melted away until a young woman with smooth, dark, ebony skin and long braids appeared. The woman flew in a circular motion above the teenagers, a thin multicolored mist resembling a rainbow exiting her mouth each time she exhaled.

Arlo stared at the angel in awe. The angel's movements alternated between rapid and slow; she flew above them like a hummingbird, but when her eyes met Arlo's, she moved slowly, like they were all underwater. The variations in speed made Arlo dizzy, and he attempted to reset his mind by closing his eyes for a few seconds, but it didn't work. Arlo looked at Isadora and realized she had the same problem; she looked distant, like she was daydreaming.

"You okay?" Arlo asked Isadora inside his mind.

"She's fine," replied a silky female voice.

Arlo looked up and saw Malaika smiling warmly at him, her eye color alternating from brown to purple.

Arlo wanted to free himself, but the strong wind kept him plastered against the ground. He opened his eyes and then closed them once more before he understood what was happening; the wind holding them down was coming from Malaika's wings. The more he tried to free himself, the faster Malaika flapped her wings. Realizing his fighting was futile, Arlo relaxed and stared at the angel. Soon, the wind from the angel's wings became as warm as a blanket, and the faint smell of cinnamon was in the air.

"And this," continued Jamison, pointing to the sky. "This is Haleena, my other sister."

Arlo and Isadora looked up and saw the shadow of an angel sitting on a dark cloud above Forneus. Suddenly, a lightning bolt lit up the sky, and Arlo saw the angel; Haleena was eerily beautiful, with blue eyes and skin so white that it was glowing. But something about her piercing blue eyes scared Arlo. Although she was an angel, he could see something evil inside Haleena; Arlo felt an immense power throbbing inside her, hovering over his soul like a boot above an ant, able to crush him at the slightest act of aggression. For the first time since he died, Arlo was truly afraid.

"If you remain civil, Forneus, I will allow you to speak," said Jamison.

Forneus mouthed the word "yes," and Jamison waved his hand in his direction.

"What do you want? Why are you here?" asked Forneus, out of breath.

Arlo was surprised at hearing Forneus's human voice - it was so deep it sounded like he was speaking from inside a well.

"We've all heard Thema speak about you; your story echoes through the Elysian fields like a nightmare, a cautionary tale of how beautiful souls can be twisted and molded into weapons against all that is good."

Forneus's eyes lit up.

"Thema?! You've seen my wife?"

"She spends most of her days mourning you. Every day, we see her walking through Heaven telling her story to anyone that will listen."

Forneus's eyes filled with tears.

"Is she healthy?"

"Pain doesn't exist in our realm."

"What was she wearing? Does she...."

Jamison motioned for Forneus to stop speaking.

"Although I pity your predicament, we are not here to lessen your pain."

Forneus's face hardened, and he wiped the tears away.

"What do you want?"

"Your recklessness has to stop."

Jamison nodded towards Arlo and Isadora lying on the ground.

"Your willingness to continuously break the laws of humanity has gotten our father's attention."

Forneus glanced at the teenagers and shrugged.

"I did what I had to do."

Jamison glared at Forneus.

"Who gave you the power to resurrect the dead?"

Forneus's nostrils flared in anger.

"You know."

"The demons of Hell took all you owned and gave you power so sinister it shakes the foundations of Heaven whenever you use it."

"Power? What power?"

Jamison smiled.

"I'm starting to understand why you're down here, and Thema lives with us in the kingdom of eternity."

Jamison turned away from Forneus and walked past Arlo and Isadora until he was facing the forest behind them. Suddenly, the ground started vibrating.

"What's that?" asked Isadora, her decaying eyes wide with fear. Arlo was about to speak when he froze - he heard the faint sounds of a child singing echoing through the forest.

"You hear that?" he asked Isadora.

"It's a child. Where is it coming from?" asked Isadora while looking around.

Soon, they discovered the source of the voice; it was coming from Jamison. Arlo and Isadora watched in astonishment as Jamison's body faded, turning gray before finally changing into a crystal-like substance. His head became transparent, and a deep purple light shone in the skull's center, pushing the light out of his eye sockets while its intensity fluctuated with the child's voice. Jamison spread his enormous transparent wings and flapped them slowly, whipping up the Cherry Blossom petals on the ground into a small tornado that encircled his body. As petals flew around him, the flame inside his glass skull grew brighter until a violet fire shot from his eyes and into the trunk of an oak tree, causing it to explode in purple fire.

Jamison backed away from the tree, and the purple light inside his glass skull faded. Slowly, his body returned to normal, and he stood watching the purple flame climbing up the tree trunk until all its leaves began burning. Suddenly, the fire shot in a zigzag through the woods, lighting the treetops of the whole forest. When purple light filled the forest, Jamison turned back to Forneus.

"The truth is light."

Suddenly, a noise rang out a few feet away from their position.

"Uhhhhhh...."

Arlo knew what it was – a zombie. Like all the others, it was high in the tree, waiting on Arlo's instructions. A few seconds passed, and then another creature moaned, then another, and another. Soon, the zombies' cries pounded Arlo's eardrums and made Isadora cover her ears.

"Make it stop," she silently mouthed while closing her eyes.

Arlo wanted to close his eyes, too. The cries made him remember he had a soul. Instead of fear, guilt overcame him, and he felt like he was shrinking away from everything. The sounds of the zombies were different now. He could hear a tortured pain within their cries like they were hurting. Their cries made him feel guilty for his part in using them - like a criminal. He had to try to comfort them.

"I'm sorry," whispered Arlo in his mind.

The words seemed to make the undead cry worse, and they started shaking the trees in protest, making purple and orange embers fly in the air like fireworks. Suddenly, thousands of sad red eyes stared at Arlo from the trees, penetrating his soul even more and making him tremble in fear. Although his eyes were white with death, they filled with tears and ran down his face. He quickly wiped them away and looked to Forneus to see if he'd noticed his moment of weakness. Arlo was surprised to see the man unaffected, rolling his eyes impatiently and looking around the forest like he didn't care.

Jamison saw Forneus's behavior and shook his head in disapproval. He calmly raised one of his palms, and the fires in the forest went out. Jamison walked over to Forneus and stood underneath him as he dangled in the air.

"I'll speak frankly, Forneus," said Jamison. "Previously, you were penalized because of your alignment with Hell. We wouldn't be here today if you had accepted your penalty and maintained your silence. But you compounded the problem."

"Compounded?"

"You raised millions from their slumber to kill for you."

"I did it to save innocent people!"

"The Angel Odessa took pity on you and granted you access to the Priming Fields to rejuvenate your soul. You sullied those sacred lands by granting access to Arlo and Isadora – two people who reeked of zombie rot when they entered."

"I felt pity for them and wanted to ease their pain!"

The Angel Haleena flew down to face Forneus with lightning shooting from her eyes in anger.

"Where is your decency? Is the truth poison on your tongue? You rejuvenated the souls of Arlo and Isadora for only one reason! Say it!"

Forneus looked away from the Angels into the forest. Haleena moved closer, her face glowing inside as the lightning bolts shot out of her eye sockets.

"Say it!" Haleena repeated.

Jamison raised his hand, and Haleena retreated to the cloud above Forneus's head.

"So you're here to kill me? Is that it?" asked Forneus.

"Our primary mission is to protect innocent souls. You've violated the rights of millions for selfish reasons, and there has to be an accounting for such treachery."

"I didn't violate anything."

"No? Look around. There is more than the death you see in the trees. It permeates the world beyond this forest, and it's spreading. It is in the streets, churches, and cemeteries – soon, death will be everywhere. Most of these people would be resting peacefully in their graves, waiting for the call of Judgment Day. You've interrupted the Sleep of Reflection, a right every deceased spirit has."

Forneus shook his head in disagreement.

"No. I brought these people back to fight. Hell is attacking, and many more innocent people will die. I had no choice but to...."

"Do you have no shame? Lies cannot shade the truth!" Jamison angrily yelled. "You used Hell's attack as a smoke screen to hide your true intentions – to reunite with your wife and son!"

"I'm not sorry about that. Why wouldn't I try to reunite with my family? I'm the victim! You knew Hell was coming for my family and did nothing to stop them!"

"It was your destiny!"

Forneus was livid.

"My destiny?! Are you serious? That demon killed my wife, raped me, and took our child to Hell!"

"Destiny's road is sometimes painful."

"Painful?! A fucking bolder fell on my head!"

"Be that as it may, each person has to endure the difficulties of their destiny. It is not your place to impose your desires on the souls of others, especially after death.

"These people you complain about would be rotting in the dirt. Why shouldn't they have a say in this world? Sure, their time here is over. But what about their families? I gave them what you didn't give me – a fighting chance."

Jamison looked at the other angels and shook his head.

"It's as Father said it would be," whispered Malaika, her eye color changing to dark blue.

Once again, Haleena drifted down from the cloud to Forneus. As he turned to look at the angel, she grabbed him by the neck and dug her long white fingernails into his flesh, causing blood to drip from his throat.

"Our father gave us orders - to wipe the souls of the sinners from the Scrolls of Life."

Haleena turned to Jamison, and the whites of her eyes became black.

"Shall I proceed?" she asked with an eerie smile.

Tears were streaming down Forneus's face.

"Fucking end it! I'm so tired of this shit!" he cried.

Jamison held up his hand.

"Not yet. We will take the most dangerous first."

Jamison turned to Arlo and Isadora.

"Me?" asked Arlo in his head. "What do you want with me?"

Jamison walked over to Arlo.

"Forneus granted you a forbidden power that was never yours to possess."

Arlo stepped back from the angel and pulled his girlfriend along with him.

"I didn't ask for this," complained Arlo.

"If we know of your power, so does Hell," continued Jamison. "We cannot risk that power falling under their control."

Isadora was afraid, and she pulled Arlo closer.

"Arlo! He's saying that...."

"What is your mission?" Arlo asked.

Jamison put his hand behind his back and pulled out a sword made of fire.

"Our father sent us here to wipe your existence from the Scrolls of Life."

4

Broken Promises

"Go in peace, you disgusting pieces of shit!"

Asura placed her hands together and closed her eyes. Soon, multiple ropes of red energy shot from her fingertips and moved along the forest floor to form a circle around a large group of Huturo. Asura jerked the strings of power, and all the monsters crashed into one another. While the confused Huturo stumbled about, another burst of energy shot from Asura's hands, and she lifted them into the air. The Huturo spotted Asura and thrashed about wildly, their eyes locked on the source of evil energy holding them captive. But Asura maintained her grip. Her old, wrinkled hands manipulated the electricity like a musical instrument, tugging slightly and pressing firmly, controlling the Huturo as they dangled in the air.

"What's the matter?" taunted Asura. "Each of you has four arms but can't break free?"

John walked over to Asura and stood behind her.

"Take it easy, Asura. Lord Balam will be angry if you hurt them," said John.

Asura turned toward her master and smiled as she struggled to hold the energy.

"Don't worry. I'm just having a little fun."

The more the Huturo struggled, the tighter Asura made their restraints. Filled with rage, some of the Huturo bit into the faces of others, spraying blood throughout the forest. Others inadvertently opened their chests to reveal the cargo they were hoarding - the heads of their victims, alive and shrieking, attached to long tentacles of meat. The victims' faces flailed about, wrapping themselves around the arms and legs of the Huturo, creating a giant ball of confusion from which none of them could escape.

As Asura strained under the weight of the group of wide-eyed creatures, thick dark veins appeared on her face and neck. Feeling weak and unsure if she could hold the Huturo any longer, she threw the ball of monsters as far as she could. The Huturo sailed over the treetops, and their screams disappeared in the storm.

With the Huturo gone, Asura turned to John.

"That was the last of the Huturo in the area. We'll only have a few minutes to initiate contact with Lord Balam before more come along," said Asura.

John walked to the center of the clearing and removed his clothing. He calmly sat in the cold mud and closed his eyes.

"Proceed."

Asura removed a small leather sack from her robe and poured the contents into her mouth. Unable to swallow all the powder, she grabbed a handful of muddy water from the ground and drank the thick liquid. The filthy sludge seemed to trigger something inside Asura; her eyes widened in surprise, and her body shook uncontrollably. Her stomach started to swell, pushing her robe outward before a deep boom sounded inside the woman, and her stomach collapsed.

"Are you okay?" asked John.

Asura threw back her head and started making strange sounds.

"Ark! Ark! Arggggh!"

Asura let one final scream escape her throat before soot began billowing out of her mouth and nose, knocking the old woman onto her back. She immediately rose to her feet, her face covered in ash and her lips trembling from her pain. John was about to help, but Asura held up her hand.

"Stay back...urgggh.... It's part of the ugggghh...."

An invisible force lifted Asura off the ground, and she started spinning in a wide circle with thick black ash billowing from her nose and mouth. Unable to breathe or speak, her eyes turned black, and liquid ash started dripping from the corners of her eyes. As she spun faster, the mud on the ground beneath her began to bubble until six shadowy hands shot up from the sludge. As Asura continued spinning, three faceless shadows climbed out of the earth. When they were out, they all turned back in John's direction and screamed. John briefly glanced at the shadows and took a deep breath before closing his eyes. The creatures turned away from John and moved closer to Asura as she spun over them. One of the creatures grabbed Asura by her legs and slammed her onto the ground. The force was so powerful that the nearby trees shook. Asura remained in a catatonic state and was unaffected by the act of aggression, her onyx-colored eyes staring up into nothingness. Another creature stood over the witch and bent over to look at her face. It raised one of its hands and dipped it into her chest. Although the creature never damaged Asura, its hand penetrated her chest like a ghost.

"Yaaaaah!" whispered Asura, her black eyes leaking more fluid.

The shadow held a beating bloody heart when it removed its hand from Asura's chest. An enormous hole opened in the shadow's face, pushing the heart muscle inside. Satisfied with its prize, the shadow backed away from Asura while another shadow climbed on top of her. Like the other shadow creature, the monster reached inside Asura's stomach and moved its hand around. When it finally found what it was searching for, it grabbed it and stood. With one violent jerk, dark brown liquid sprayed everywhere, and the creature began pulling out Asura's intestines like a rope. With one hand over another, the shadow pulled Asura's entrails out until there was nothing more to remove. After tugging on Asura's guts to make sure her guts were secure, it released the intestines, and the long rope of flesh remained suspended in the air aimed at John. With one final shriek, all three creatures dove into the ground and disappeared.

"Sahkeli-do-kila, Sahkeli-do-kila," chanted Asura, her mouth thick with mud.

Excrement shot out of Asura's intestines in a spray, covering John's body. John remained unfazed by the fluid; he calmly wiped the gunk off his eyelids with two fingers and lay down on the ground.

"Sahkeli-do-kila," continued Asura. "Sahkeli-do-kila."

Asura's chanting abruptly stopped. Thunder began rumbling overhead, and the wind started blowing furiously.

"Do you accept the keys of Hell?" a voice whispered.

John recognized the voice and ground his teeth in fear.

"I do," he replied.

Without warning, a thick patch of skin lifted off John's stomach.

"Ah!" screamed John.

The skin removal from his stomach surprised John; he recalled the last time Lord Balam ripped off his skin – it was part of the process; no earthly being could see a demon without an offering of flesh. But the process felt different this time, more personal.

When the invisible force snatched the skin off his left arm, it tore off more than his skin – it ripped out the veins in his forearm.

"Ahhhh! Please!" screamed John as blood sprayed everywhere.

He immediately tried to stop the bleeding by placing his arm over the wound. But he felt the skin on his shoulders torn away, this time exposing his bare shoulders.

John's calm demeanor transformed into unbridled fear. His eyes widened like a horse's, revealing his fear of the demon's power.

"Ahhhhh!" he screamed.

The torture became gruesome – the force started slowly pulling out the hair on John's scalp, each follicle tearing chunks of flesh from his head. Bubbles appeared on John's stomach, growing like giant cherry blood-filled orbs until each globule popped, dripping stomach acid down his waist, causing blisters to form. His testicles began to swell until they exploded, and the skin on his privates sizzled like bacon on fire. When John felt the skin torn from the bottom of his feet, he was delirious with pain and started vomiting blood on himself.

"M-my Lord," John begged while shaking uncontrollably. " I'm your f-faithful s-servant...."

There was a strong gust of wind, and the assault on John's body stopped. Slowly, John raised his bloody skinless head and looked around.

"You have failed me," came a deep female voice at his feet.

John tried lifting himself on his elbows.

"Ahhhh!" he screamed, the burning pain knocking him back into the mud.

Soon, a beautifully hideous woman leaned over him.

"You knew the penalty."

John could do nothing but wince in pain and stare at his master. It was the first time he'd seen Balam without her cloak. Balam was beautiful and terrifying. She was a shapeshifter that changed her appearance every few seconds, appearing as a gorgeous, voluptuous naked woman before transforming into a towering five-eyed demon with leathery red skin and two large horns sitting atop her head.

"Your mistakes have cost us thousands of new souls."

Balam extended one long finger and ran it along John's left ear. Suddenly, his ear became a pile of glowing red ants, and they all rushed into John's earhole.

"Ahhhh! Please! Ahhhhh!" screamed John.

John temporarily forgot his other ailments. He could feel the ants burrowing deep inside his ear canal, ripping off chunks of flesh as they moved steadily toward their destination – his brain.

"Please, Master! The Angels interfered! I tried to - AAAAAHHHH!"

Suddenly, the right side of John's face turned a deep red.

"Please, Lord! Give me another chance!"

John's face started glowing, and he started choking on his tongue. He could feel the ants burrowing into the optical nerve of his left eye. The back of John's head went numb, and the world around him became a distortion of colors and sounds. After a few moments, his left eye burst into flame.

"Why should we give you another chance?"

"Because I can convince Arlo to give you what you want!"

Balam lifted her hand, and the fire on John's face disappeared.

"I'm listening."

With his body spasming in pain, John tried to explain.

"Arlo now has the power to control the undead."

Balam became angry and waved her arm over John's body, causing it to burst into flame.

"Do not waste my time with things we already know!"

"Okay, my Lord! I'll tell you!"

The demon waved her hand again, and the fire went out.

"Asura discovered the spell the Witches of Blood Mountain used to give Arlo control of the zombies. Heaven forbids the spell, and the punishment for using it is immediate removal from the Scrolls of Life."

Balam turned to John and smiled.

"Interesting. So the Angels are not here because of the Huturo?"

"No, my Lord. The Angels are here to kill Arlo and wipe his family from the Scrolls of Life."

"And Arlo is unaware of this?"

"I don't think he knows."

"It will be difficult to convince the boy that Heaven is his true enemy."

"Yes, my Lord. But we have the upper hand."

"Explain."

"We have Arlo's mother."

Balam's smiled deviously.

"Where is she?"

"Unconscious in the cave."

Balam looked in the direction of the cave while John continued speaking.

"We can show Arlo that Heaven is trying to kill him and his family. Meanwhile, we can gain his trust by showing him we protected his mother. By revealing Heaven's plot, Arlo might be willing to join us."

Balam shook her head.

"We want the mother's soul too."

Fearing Balam would attack him again, John began to stutter.

"L-lord, I'm not saying we must give Claire to Arlo. B-But he'll join us if he believes she's safe and we acted in his family's best interest. Once he agrees, we can control the zombies through Arlo and use them to capture the children. After Arlo gives you his soul, you can kill Claire and take her soul too."

Balam transformed into a naked woman and lowered her face close to John's. Slowly, a long, forked tongue covered in maggots shot out of her mouth and licked his bloody face.

"I'm impressed."

John tried smiling, but the burns on his face were too painful.

"I'm here to serve you, my Lord."

Balam transformed back into the monster, her red skin shimmering as if covered in a glaze of blood.

"Are you sure you want to serve by my side in the fires of Hell?"

John tried to smile again.

"Yes, Lord. I want that more than anything!"

Balam threw back her head and laughed. The demon's laughter made John shiver in fear; he heard three demonic voices inside the monster.

"You have not proven your worthiness to serve by my side."

"Please, Lord! I can do this! Give me another chance."

"If you fail us again, I'll take you to The Supreme One, and he'll feast on your soul."

"I won't fail. You'll see."

Balam closed her eyes, and her body transformed into a woman. Slowly, her image began to fade.

"My Lord! Wait!"

"Speak."

"The Huturo and the Feasters are becoming a problem for me. Although we share the same mission, they attack us."

"Is the witch Asura unable to protect you?"

"Yes, Lord Balam. But with the Angels, it's...."

Balam held up her hand, and John stopped speaking.

"At midnight on the third day, I will send reinforcements."

Balam finally disappeared. As John lay on the table panting and crying in pain, he heard a splash on the ground beside him. John turned and saw Asura lying on her back in the mud with her intestines hanging from her stomach. After a few seconds, he heard her panting and moaning in pain.

5

When They Come For Us

Arlo and Isadora backed away from the angel as he moved closer with his flaming sword.

"I don't understand," said Arlo in his head. "We're the victims!"

Jamison lifted the sword, making the teenagers cower in fear as they felt the heat from the blade warming their bodies.

"Although the decision to wipe you from the Scrolls of Life is not ours, it is just. Your continued existence is a contamination on the souls of the innocent that Heaven cannot allow."

Isadora began growling, her eyes glowing red with anger. With thick saliva dripping from the hole in her face, she snarled at Jamison.

"You're no better than the demons that invaded our lives. I hope you all burn in Hell for this."

Just as Jamison raised the sword to kill Arlo, Arlo sent a mental command to the zombies hiding in the forest.

"Attack!"

There was a collective shriek, and suddenly, hundreds of zombies flew through the air. Arlo saw this as his best opportunity to flee; he grabbed Isadora's hand, and they ran into the dark forest. Just as they did, a man with half his face missing fell from the treetops while a skeleton with a skull covered in thin gray hair sprinted out of the shadows, screaming.

A dead child with pale bluish-white skin ran toward Jamison, its chin covered in fresh maggots.

Jamison seemed unaffected by the onslaught. He calmly stepped to his right, and the monster child ran past him and crashed into a tree. Jamison lifted the sword to kill Arlo, but dozens of zombies jumped between Jamison and the teenagers, knocking the kids into the mud before turning to the angel.

The zombie attack surprised the other angels. After watching from the sky, Malaika and Haleena descended on Jamison's position. Malaika pushed at the air with her open palm, and dozens of zombies fell to the ground. Haleena was more vicious with her attack; after running her hand along the blade of her sword and changing it to a jagged knife, she tossed the weapon into the air and sent the blade spinning through the woods, chopping up the zombies like a buzzsaw. Several zombies ducked the sword and ran at her, but Haleena became angrier and formed balls of white light with her hands. She hurled the orbs of light into the creatures' faces, stripping the flesh from their skulls and igniting their bodies in white fire. With their heads stripped of meat and their bodies burning, the zombies fell to the ground, shrieking in pain, burning until they were piles of ash.

"Haleena! Restrain yourself! These are innocents."

Haleena frowned at Jamison before waving her hand again; the balls of light returned to her palm, and she caught the sword and sheathed it. As soon as she did, another hoard of zombies burst from the darkness, and she pushed her hand toward the group, knocking them on their backs.

Two zombies rushed Malaika - the angel smiled as they approached before calmly flapping her wings to send them flying over the treetops. When another wave of monsters emerged, Jamison raised his palm and spoke to them.

"Wait," said Jamison. "We are only after Arlo."

But the creatures only briefly paused before rushing toward the group of angels. This time, a bald, overweight, middle-aged man with a hole in his chest ran toward Jamison. Before the man reached the angel, he grabbed a skeleton crawling in the mud and hurled it at Jamison. The angel didn't duck this time – he opened his robe, and a burst of white light flooded the forest. The skeleton went inside Jamison's chest and disappeared. The fat man paused, looking around, unsure of how to proceed. Finally, the zombie ran forward, but before he reached Jamison, the man fell to the ground and stopped moving. Suddenly, there was a great rush in the trees around them, and the remaining zombies started falling to the ground.

"What did you do, Jamison?" asked Malaika.

Jamison walked to the zombies and kneeled to look at the lifeless creatures.

"He's running," replied Jamison.

Jamison turned to Haleena.

"Take Forneus."

Haleena smiled and looked at Forneus as he dangled in the sky. She happily unsheathed her sword of fire and flew up to him.

"Hell has my son. What will become of him?"

Haleena grabbed Forneus's neck. She pulled him close as he struggled within her grasp and whispered in his ear.

"Hell has your son now, and we can't reach him until he surfaces. But don't worry. We'll wipe him from the Scrolls of Life as soon as he appears."

Forneus sobbed.

"Please! There has to be another way. What about my wife?"

Jamison flew up to Forneus. A sadness overcame him as he hovered in the sky beside the man's ghostly image. He felt sorry for Forneus.

"She made it to Heaven before your indiscretions. Don't worry. Your wife is safe."

The words seemed to comfort Forneus, and he relaxed. After a few moments, Jamison nodded to Haleena, and she slid the blade across Forneus's neck. Forneus immediately grabbed his throat, feeling for the wound.

"It didn't work! Thank God!"

Forneus and Haleena flew down and landed beside Forneus's bones.

"Wow! Thank you so much for giving me another chance!" Forneus's ghost said as it faded.

Suddenly, an explosion was on the ground, and the angels saw a black flame rising from Forneus's bones.

Malaika kneeled by the black flame and began speaking.

"Silence is beauty. Pass away."

The three angels stood watching the flame until it was gone.

6

Swallowed

Claire peered out of the bushes, looking for anything that seemed familiar.

"Where am I?" she whispered.

The rain was heavy, tapping her scalp like icy fingers before dripping down her forehead into her eyes. Claire wiped the rain away and tucked her hair behind her ears.

"Everything's going to be okay," Claire whispered.

But inside, she was a panicked mess. Claire was lost and didn't know where she was. Worse, she could hear sounds in the forest, grunting and growling from bizarre things as they tore through the woods.

Earlier, Claire heard footsteps and became excited about being found. But just as the footsteps drew near, it occurred to Claire that those footsteps could belong to her captors. She quickly dove behind a bush and hid, watching to see what was approaching. Claire almost screamed when she got a look at the monster; the four-armed creature looked like a dead person resurrected. Its enormous eyes shimmered in the rain like diamonds as it laughed like a child. It looked in Claire's direction – she could tell it picked up her scent and was moving to destroy her.

But suddenly, a giant black bear emerged from the shadows. It saw the four-armed monster and rushed it, growling as it swiped at the creature with its razor-sharp claws. The monster giggled gleefully before attacking the bear. With two arms, it grabbed the monster's neck and held the animal in place while its other arms grabbed handfuls of the bear's fat on its belly. With one mighty thrust, it tore open the bear's stomach, causing its intestines to hang out of the openings. The bear bellowed in agony, but the monster grabbed another handful of belly and tore again. Before the bear collapsed, Claire had taken advantage of the murderous distraction and ran off, hiding in the shadows until she was clear of the creature. And now she was lost in the forest, trying to find her way home.

Claire stood motionless, listening. After a few seconds, she cautiously stepped out from the shadows and continued her journey. The forest floor felt like a sponge; it squished and tugged, trying to remove her shoes as Claire stepped. Claire was so tired, yet she pushed herself to continue.

Suddenly, a bolt of lightning tore across the sky, and Claire jumped; seconds later, thunder rumbled the ground beneath her feet, and the sound of howling monsters rose from the darkness.

"They're close," whispered Claire.

She could tell it was more than one monster, dozens, maybe. They tore at the trees as they moved, growling in the darkness. Claire gauged where the monsters were and cut a wide circle to avoid them. When the monsters' growling grew faint, she pushed toward the area she believed was nearest to the city.

Claire continued walking uninterrupted. Soon, she pushed through a set of bushes, and something moved in a nearby group of shrubs, freezing Claire in her tracks. Terrified, she watched the bushes, waiting. A tiny brown fox exited the bushes. After staring at Claire, the little creature ran past her and disappeared.

Claire continued pushing through the woods. Soon, memories of her family began tormenting her; she remembered being wrapped in her husband Jamie's embrace in front of the crackling fireplace while her son Arlo sat quietly in the recliner, scribbling poems. Her life, only a few weeks removed from her current predicament, had been as close to perfect as Claire could hope. And now it was gone, replaced by a strange, terrifying world she didn't understand.

Claire had seen unexplainable, murderous creatures that should only live in nightmares. She didn't want to believe the monsters she saw in the hospital existed, but the buzz of flies, the piles of corpses littering the hospital floor, and the disgusting odor were too strong to ignore. Claire tried telling herself she was drugged and possibly suffered a head injury. But deep down, Claire always knew the truth – she wasn't crazy, and the things she saw were real.

Claire arrived at a new set of shrubbery and stopped. After ensuring nothing was around, she pushed aside a large leaf and walked through, only to arrive at a new wall of foliage – one that she was sure she'd visited before.

"Shit!" cursed Claire.

She was tired and cold. As her breath clouded in front of her face, Claire felt the weight of fatigue on her shoulders. The freezing rain stuck to her skin like a thin ice sheet, adding to her depression. Claire wanted to sleep so badly but knew she couldn't stop. She was sure the witch was aware of her absence by now, and Claire had to get as far away as possible. Claire turned and looked into a different part of the forest. She didn't know where she was, but she had to keep moving. Suddenly, a child's scream echoed through the woods, and Claire looked around.

"Manuel or John?" Claire whispered.

The names opened a floodgate of questions in Claire's mind. Manuel had been her son Arlo's friend for years. Why was he now answering to the name John? Who was this woman with him? Where was Manuel's family?

Suddenly, Claire's stomach growled, and she doubled over in pain. She had been so busy with everything that she didn't realize she hadn't eaten in three days. Claire quickly scanned the nearby bushes when her eyes fell on a strange plant growing at the base of a tree; several medium-sized red berries were hanging from a thick vine that wrapped around the tree trunk. With her mouthwatering and her knees shaking, Claire walked over to the plant and fell to her knees. Claire reached out to grab the fruit and paused, trying to remember the lessons she had learned in summer camp as a child about how to identify poisonous plants. But her mind was too foggy with hunger. Claire moved closer to inspect the plant; the vines covering the tree trunk were black, but as they got closer to the fruit, they became a translucent pinkish color, and Claire could see liquid moving inside.

"What the hell?" asked Claire.

She grew nervous and was about to turn away when a flower near one of the pieces of fruit opened, and a pink mist rose. Suddenly, the smell of fresh strawberries filled the air. Claire couldn't control herself - she reached out and plucked one of the pieces of fruit from the vine. As soon as she did, the fruit burst between thumb and forefinger.

"Shit!" she whispered.

Claire was about to drop the open fruit to the ground when a thick black bug covered in horns scampered out of the fruit onto Claire's hand and bit off her thumb. As blood sprayed from her open wound, the bug fell to the ground and scurried into the bushes.

"Whaaa..." said Claire stumbling back.

She stood dazed for a few seconds, unable to register what had happened. Backing away from the strange plant, she turned around and realized she was standing in the middle of an area filled with the deadly fruit. As the blood sprayed from her thumbless hand, the gravity of her predicament set in, and she screamed.

"Ahhhhh!"

Suddenly, the fruit around her exploded, and dozens of insects rushed at her from all sides. Claire clutched her bleeding hand and backed away, tripping over a log and crashing to the ground. She immediately rose to her feet and tried to run, but the creatures blocked her path. Claire looked to her right and found an even larger group of monster bugs rushing at her from the patches - their red, beady eyes focused on the blood dripping from her hand.

Realizing the path behind her was the only option for escape, Claire took off running, scratching her face on a large briar. But she didn't have time to worry about the injury. Claire was cold and losing so much blood that she knew it wouldn't be long before she passed out. Claire ran through a group of bushes and turned – Claire didn't know where she was, and everything was black. Claire turned right, then left. Finally, she burst through a large bush and almost crashed face-first into a tree with the strange fruit all over it.

"Oh, my God," she whispered, slowly backing away from the bulbs.

The fruit began pulsating and bubbling, oozing a thick, clear liquid as the tentacles of the monster inside poked through the fruit. Soon, their hideous faces appeared with glowing red eyes, causing the fruit to glow from the inside. Suddenly, a hole opened in the fruit, and one of the demonic creatures emerged, and then two more, all hissing and emitting a strange buzz. Claire backed away, holding her injured hand, but the voracious bugs spotted Claire's blood, excitedly ripped apart the fruit and ran towards her; their lightbulb-shaped heads filled with jagged teeth snapping as they approached.

Claire tried backing away and bumped into something soft and sticky. She tried turning around but couldn't move – whatever was behind Claire held her shirt. With one mighty thrust, Claire pulled herself free and turned around. When she saw what was holding her, she froze in disbelief – she was face to face with one of the vampire creatures, a bald, naked woman with dozens of suctioning mouths all over her body.

"Ahhhhh!" Claire screamed.

The woman tried reaching out to grab Claire but couldn't move her arms; some invisible force held her back. The creature snarled, the mouths on its faces sucking, trying to taste Claire's face. Claire crept steadily back with a watchful eye for the pile of demonic insects at her flank. The vampire monster began grunting, trying to free itself, but could not. The beast finally lunged at Claire and came within inches of her face.

"No!" Claire screamed.

As Claire turned to run, a hand shot out of the shadows and grabbed her throat.

"Where do you think you're going?"

Claire watched as Asura stepped out of the shadows, her wrinkled face stained with blood. The witch held Claire in a vicelike grip with one hand while extending her open palm in the vampire's direction, restraining it with her black magic.

"Please," begged Claire. "I n-need to get to...."

Asura lowered her hand and turned her back on the monster. Just as the creature attacked, Asura's eyes became black, and the creature's body exploded, covering Claire in the vampire's blood. Claire tried to run away but only took a few steps before Asura grabbed her by the throat again.

As Claire struggled to break free, John stepped out from behind Asura. His appearance startled Claire; the skin on his face was red and bleeding as if he'd been in a fire.

"Hi, Mrs. Ortega. It wasn't nice of you to sneak off like that."

"Please! I need to get to a doctor!"

Claire shoved her thumbless hand in front of John's face, and John smiled.

"I'm not surprised. There are dangerous creatures in this forest."

Asura grabbed Claire's injured hand and held it tight. Terrified, Claire tried pulling away, but Asura held firm.

"De-luni-targ-tuoi," chanted Asura.

Suddenly, Claire's hand started tingling.

"What are you doing?" she asked. "Get off me!"

"Relax, Mrs. Ortega. We're trying to help you," said John.

Claire became angry.

"You tell this crazy bitch to let go of my hand right now!" screamed Claire.

"Look into my eyes," whispered Asura.

Claire looked into Asura's dark eyes and suddenly felt an excruciating pain radiating across her hand.

"Ow! Let me go, you crazy bitch!"

Claire tried looking at her hand but discovered she couldn't move her head; the witch had her locked in a spell, unable to stop staring into Asura's eyes. Claire became sleepy, and her breathing slowed.

"Please...L-let me go," she whispered as her eyelids grew heavy.

Claire's entire body was warm now. She swayed back and forth in a hypnotic trance, staring into the eyes of Asura.

"What...is....she....doing?"

John moved closer to Claire and smiled.

"Are you relaxed?"

Claire shook her head.

"Please, I want to sleep now."

"Not yet, Mrs. Ortega."

Claire smiled as small droplets of sweat appeared on her forehead.

"Okay."

John placed two fingers on Claire's bottom lip.

"Are you ready?"

Claire smiled.

"Ready for what?" she asked.

Suddenly, John grabbed the back of Claire's head. With one forceful movement, he shoved his hand inside Claire's mouth until it reached the back of Claire's throat.

"Argggh," gagged Claire, her eyes still focused on Asura's.

Claire snapped out of her trance and opened her eyes. She was standing alone in the middle of blackness, and there was no light or ground, only her breathing echoing.

"Hello?" yelled Claire.

The sound of her voice returned in a horrible echo, accompanied by the sound of deep demonic laughter.

"Manuel?" she called. "Where are you?"

Once again, Claire's voice echoed back to her with the sinister laugh underneath.

Claire's hand was hurting so much that she tried to raise it to look, but she couldn't see anything but darkness.

"Manuel!" she called again.

Suddenly, Claire had a thought.

"John!" she whispered.

"Now you know us," boomed a deep voice.

The voice was even more terrifying than the echoes.

"Where am I?"

"You are here with all of us."

"All of us?"

Suddenly, a light flashed, and Claire saw hundreds of monsters surrounding her. The creatures were covered in blood, clawing at one another and biting chunks of flesh from each other's bodies as they reached for her.

"Ahhhhh!" she screamed.

The light went out, and once again, Claire was in darkness. Suddenly she felt a cold finger touch her shoulder and she jumped.

"Whose there?"

But there was only silence. With wide eyes, Claire turned around in circles as she scanned the darkness. Suddenly, another finger touched her leg.

"Ahhhhh!" screamed Claire. "Stop! Please!"

The same deep voice laughed at Claire.

"John? Is that you?" asked Claire. "Please! Get me out of here!"

The voice didn't respond.

"John? Are you there?"

"We will help you under one condition."

"Anything! Just get me out of here!"

"We ask for your help convincing your son to join us."

Claire stopped shaking.

"Is that why I'm here? Because of Arlo?"

"Do you agree to help us?"

Suddenly, Claire's fear melted away, and she became angry. Although monsters surrounded her, all Claire could see was the old woman's manipulative face standing behind John. Did that old bitch think she was stupid enough to betray her child? Claire started to doubt the images of the monsters, the cold hands reaching out to touch her from the darkness. She now believed the old woman had slipped her a drug, causing her to hallucinate.

"It all makes sense now," she whispered.

Since Claire had been with the two of them, she'd seen things that didn't make sense: strange plants, monstrous creatures, something she could not reconcile with reality. Now, John's question glued everything together. The old lady was at the bottom of it. Why would a child want to be referred to by a name that wasn't his? Now John was trying to get her to lie to Arlo? The question he asked now made her almost sure of her theory – the old woman gave him drugs, and now she wanted to get Arlo involved.

"Well?" boomed the deep voice. "What is your answer?"

Claire kept her anger hidden and spoke in a calm, even tone.

"Yes, I'll help you. Just get me out of this place."

The voice laughed. Suddenly, there was a flash of light, and Claire was back in the rainy forest, standing in front of the boy and the old woman.

"Look at your hand," said John.

Claire raised her hand, and her mouth fell open – her thumb had grown back!

"I don't understand. How did you do this?" asked Claire.

John and Asura ignored her question and started walking away.

"Come with us, Mrs. Ortega. Many strange creatures are in this forest, and you won't make it out alone."

John took Claire's hand and gently pulled her arm. Claire spotted more strange fruit on a tree a few feet away. Reluctantly, she followed John and Asura.

7

New Dead

As Arlo and Isadora sprinted through the forest, they continued to look nervously behind in search of the pursuing Angels.

"Where are they?" asked Isadora inside her mind.

Arlo didn't respond; he was too busy transmitting the same command repeatedly to the hoard of zombies around them.

Protect us! Run to the city!

Suddenly, a pair of Huturo jumped out from the darkness; they saw the teenagers and paused, staring at the couple, seemingly confused. Before the monsters attacked, zombies sprinted out of the brush and jumped on top of the creatures, holding them down until Arlo and Isadora ran clear.

Arlo and Isadora continued running, expecting the angels to appear at any moment. But the only sound was those of the hoard of zombies tearing apart trees as they cleared a path for the teenagers to escape.

"The angels aren't following us. Can we slow down?"

Arlo didn't hear Isadora and continued pulling her through the forest. He wasn't thinking about the angels that hunted him, nor the death of Forneus. Arlo could only think of one thing - human brains. Although he'd eaten enough animal flesh to stave off the fires of the Sun Oil, he couldn't take his mind off killing the man in the cabin. The man's brains were so sweet and slimy as they slid down his throat. Eating the brains filled his body with an energy that couldn't be reproduced by consuming the animals in the forest. Human brains tasted different, more delicious, and Arlo wanted them now.

Suddenly, Isadora stopped running and doubled over.

"What is it?" asked Arlo.

Isadora's body spasmed, and she almost knocked him over.

"I... I..."

Isadora couldn't finish her thought. Something was pushing from inside her chest, and the bones in her spine were cracking.

"Ahhhh!" she moaned in a demonic voice.

Suddenly, Isadora raised her arms. Arlo watched as an invisible force yanked his girlfriend's arms, pulling them behind her until they popped out of their sockets.

"Grrrrr!" growled Isadora as her head jerked from side to side.

Unable to lift her dislocated arms, she dropped to her knees and growled.

"Isadora," Arlo said softly. *"What's happening?"*

Arlo grabbed a handful of Isadora's hair and jerked her head back. He recoiled when he saw his girlfriend's face. Isadora's white eyes leaked a green substance, and a big black pulsating blister was on her left temple. Part of Isadora's nose was missing, and a thick black substance was dripping from her nasal cavity.

But Isadora's physical changes didn't scare Arlo as much as what he didn't see; Isadora's personality was gone. All he knew of his girlfriend was absent; the warmth of her soul radiating through her decaying body, wit, thoughtfulness, and sense of humor were all gone and replaced with a sinister hunger and unquenchable fury. She didn't appear conscious; it was as though something filled her with rage and released her into a world of darkness.

"Braaains!" she moaned in a deep demonic voice.

Isadora tossed her head about wildly in search of victims.

"Braaains," she begged again as thick green spit poured from her mouth.

"What's happening to us? It's like we...."

Arlo couldn't finish his thought. Suddenly, an invisible force grabbed his head and twisted it in the opposite direction until it broke. Arlo wanted to scream but couldn't. The scent of brains was so strong that it overpowered all his senses.

"Braaaains," he begged.

Arlo jerked his head from side to side, ignoring the rattling of broken bones in his neck as he searched for the source of the aroma, but he could not find anyone. Suddenly, his stomach spasmed, and he threw up all the animal meat he'd eaten.

"Braaaains," Arlo moaned. "Please... Braaaains..."

He no longer cared about Isadora and said nothing when she rose to her feet and stumbled forward. Instead, Arlo continued searching the forest; the smell of brains was everywhere, making the teenagers run in all directions, ripping apart the forest. But they couldn't find any victims.

Without realizing it, Arlo sent a mental command to the other zombies in the forest.

Brains! Kill all! Search everywhere!

Suddenly, the zombies were everywhere; dozens of undead rushed out of the darkness, screaming like furious monsters, ripping saplings from the ground while pushing through the forest for brains. Another group of zombies ran to Isadora and grabbed her, but after sniffing her skull, they dropped her and ran off. Arlo was confused and immediately ran to her side.

"Isadora," he said, trying to lift his girlfriend off the ground.

Isadora's only response was aggression.

"Grrrrr!" she growled.

Isadora jumped to her feet, pushed Arlo aside, and sniffed the air. Detecting the smell of brains, she scattered up a tree, climbed onto the edge of a thin branch, and started smelling.

"Please... Braaaains..." Isadora begged.

Suddenly, the tree branch gave way, and Isadora crashed to the ground. Arlo ran to Isadora to see if she was okay, but he picked up a new whiff of human brains nearby and sprinted into the brush.

"Braaains," he said, tossing aside briars.

Arlo heard his voice this time, and a new wave of terror washed over him - he didn't recognize the deep voice yelling for brains; it sounded childlike, like a lost child calling for his mother.

Zombies were everywhere. The soft rainy ground was now a mud pit with hundreds of the undead clawing at one another – all searching for brains. Arlo and Isadora were part of the hoard, each picking up on the scent of brains that eluded them all. Isadora's mind was gone, while Arlo's thoughts alternated between madness and the tiny piece of humanity that existed only a few hours ago. A dead woman in a ragged wedding dress appeared before Arlo, her eyes glowing in the night rain. Arlo rushed her and grabbed her throat. He was about to sink his teeth into her scalp when the bitter scent of death shot up his nose like ammonia. Arlo dropped the woman and turned away, attempting to find the smell of brains in the air again. Just as he did, two dead children, one missing an arm and the other missing half its face, rushed Arlo. The zombie children jumped on Arlo's chest and were about to bite his head when they suddenly fell off and ran away, screaming into the forest.

As Arlo lay on his back with madness surrounding him, he regained part of his sanity and looked around. All the zombies were fleeing the mud pit, scattering into the forest. Confused, Arlo rolled onto his stomach and looked behind - a golden silhouette was floating high above the trees. Arlo transmitted a message to the zombies:

The Angels are here! Hide!

Most zombies saw the angels and ran away before Arlo warned them, but the others who hadn't seen the silhouette seemed confused. They looked around, screaming and grunting before spotting the angels and running away in fear.

Arlo spotted Isadora lying in the mud puddle, ran to her, and lifted her off the ground. He tried to pull her into the bushes, but as soon as they took a few steps, another glowing angelic figure stepped into their path. Arlo reached for Isadora's waist, but his hand slipped into the gaping wound on her side and disappeared into her internal organs. Isadora responded to the bodily invasion like a cat.

"Hissssss!"

Arlo ignored her protest, quickly removed his hand from her torso, and grabbed her arm. After sidestepping the figure, he pursued another escape path, but there was nowhere to run.

"Grrrrr!" growled Arlo.

Arlo tried calling the zombies to come to his aid.

"P-p-p..."

Arlo let go of Isadora's arm and pounded his head in frustration – he couldn't remember the words!

Suddenly, the sky lit up, casting a brilliant light throughout the forest. As Arlo and Isadora recoiled, the figures moved closer, and Arlo could see their faces. It was the three angels.

"The suffering you are experiencing is intentional," said Jamison, extending his wings.

Jamison flew across the forest floor and landed in front of Arlo and Isadora as they crouched.

"Forneus spoiled you with a power that was not his to give. I've removed that power to allow you to experience the real pain you caused."

Hallena stepped out of the shadows and unsheathed her sword of fire. With a watchful eye on Arlo, she moved to cut off the nearest path of escape.

"You will not escape, sinner," whispered Haleena.

Jamison moved closer.

"Forgive my sister's harsh words. She only wants to stop the suffering of the innocent."

Arlo forced himself to speak.

"N-not.... our f-f-fault."

Jamison smiled.

"It is not our position to pass judgment on you, Arlo. We are only here following orders."

Malaika opened her wings, jumped over the group, and landed behind them, a calm expression on her face.

"We don't want to do this," said Malaika in a velvety voice. "But the pain has to stop."

Jamison pulled out his sword of fire.

"The hunger you feel and the nagging inside your mind for Hell's nourishment of forbidden flesh goes against all that is good. These souls you control with your mind are your brothers and sisters, and they deserve peace, not to be weapons of sin. Forneus gave no forethought about the impact of his selfish decision. He lied to you and shielded you from the truth of what he was doing. He taught you how to evade the natural correction of Sun Oil. He gave you access to the Priming Fields, a sacred place meant for the peaceful preparation of souls before entering the ever-after. Now, that place is forever soiled with the rot of sin. Like it or not, both of you played a part in that. For these reasons and many more, our father has sent us here to correct the error of Forneus."

"Y-you will kill us?" asked Arlo with his voice, his throat filled with the phlegm of the dead.

"We will remove you and your bloodline from the Scrolls of Life," replied Jamison.

Suddenly, Isadora began grunting and shaking her head. Slowly, she started piecing together a sentence.

"Y-you will...{grrr} kill our f-families? T-they are innocent."

Malaika moved close to Isadora and touched the girl's head.

"Now speak."

Isadora's white eyes became brown, and she started speaking without difficulty.

"What about our mothers and fathers? You will take them too?"

Jamison shook his head.

"You are a victim, child. We are not here for you."

Isadora looked at Arlo and started crying.

"I don't understand, Arlo. They're here to kill you?"

Arlo stood and started backing away.

"Heaven is supposed to be about love and forgiveness," complained Isadora. "This isn't love!"

Jamison's eyes filled with tears.

"It is my father's demand."

Isadora grew angry.

"I won't let you take him! I love Arlo!"

"You don't have a choice."

Isadora turned to face Arlo.

"I love you, Arlo. I won't let them take you!"

Arlo sighed and shook his head.

"It's okay, Isadora. I love you too. Try not to forget me."

"We are not messengers of peace, Arlo. We are warriors."

Jamison nodded to Haleena. The angel stood before Arlo and raised the sword of fire above her head. Just as Haleena was about to strike Arlo, Isadora pushed Arlo out of the way.

"No!" screamed Isadora.

The blade of fire missed Arlo entirely but struck Isadora on top of her head. Red sparks shot everywhere as the sword moved through her head, neck, and torso, cutting Isadora's body in half.

"Haleena!" screamed Malaika. "You've wiped an innocent from the Scrolls!"

Haleena stood transfixed; she stared at Isadora's body in shock, unable to believe what she'd done.

"No.... no.....no...." she whispered, her eyes filled with tears.

"I-I didn't mean to...."

Jamison glanced at Arlo's face and saw fury rising within him. He thought about using his sword to kill Arlo before he responded but couldn't bring himself to do it; Haleena had hurt the boy so much that Jamison felt pity for him. Jamison grabbed Haleena's arm and pulled her back.

"Get away from him!" he whispered, focusing on Arlo.

Arlo watched as the fire from Haleena's blade burned Isadora's skin. As the stench of her intestines rose in the air, a wave of fury overcame Arlo.

"Noooooo!"

Arlo heard something pounding in his head, a deep booming drum that made everything around him vibrate. He knew what it was – his anger, and Arlo welcomed it, called upon it to punish those who took his friend. Soon, his chest was burning, and Arlo fell to his knees.

"Kill everything!" said Arlo in his mind.

Malaika sensed something terrible was about to happen and shot into the sky, leaving Jamison and Haleena to face Arlo's fury. The other angels tried to fly away, but before they could leave the ground, Arlo's voice shot through the forest like a bomb. Trees splintered, and boulders cracked while the angels tumbled through the woods like rag dolls. Jamison rose to his feet and checked on Haleena before returning to Arlo.

"Arlo! Calm down! Something's happening to you!"

But Arlo didn't listen. The anger he felt pushed him in ways he'd never felt. He wanted to dance on the corpses of the angels, bathe in their blood, and chew on their cold hearts.

"You killed her for nothing!"

Arlo felt death everywhere, in the trees and the ground beneath him. He felt the souls of the dead begging for freedom from their tombs. Somehow, Arlo could feel the death in all the world, all the anger and sadness of the millions of people who died prematurely; they were all talking to him now. Their cries of pain filled every part of his body and soul, and Arlo wanted them to be free.

Unable to hold the power building inside him, Arlo released a powerful scream that tore the feathers from Jamison's wings and sent him flying. Jamison crashed into a large oak tree and fell to the ground with cartilage and bone hanging from his back, the only remnants of his mighty wings. With golden liquid pouring from his mouth, Jamison climbed to his knees.

"Malaika! Haleena!" screamed Jamison. "Get away! He's becoming the Akuji Zār!"

Malaika turned to face Arlo and held up her hands.

"Please, Arlo. Try to regain control of yourself. Isadora's demise was an accident."

Arlo glanced at Isadora's split corpse; half of her body lay face-down in the mud with the intestines spilling out, while the other half lay empty, the face cauterized and bruised with her one eye staring at him. The gruesome imagery filled Arlo's eyes with tears, and his knees shook. He stared at Isadora's torn body and saw love, his girlfriend. He remembered the time they'd shared in the Priming Fields, her face so innocent and pure, the taste of fresh peaches as he kissed her lips. All of that was gone now, taken away by the angels. They were liars carrying messages of love and protection, but Isadora's torn body held the truth about who they were - killers of the last person that mattered.

"Die!" Arlo shouted inside his mind.

Arlo slammed his hands into the mud, and the ground started trembling. Malaika and Haleena tried flew around trying to anticipate what was coming, but a colossal tree knocked them to the ground. They quickly pushed the tree off and stumbled about until they finally regained their balance. With a burst of wind, they took off high into the stormy sky.

"I loved her!" cried Arlo as tears streamed down his face.

He pushed his arms deeper into the soil, and the ground started bubbling around the forest. Jamison saw tiny white objects pushing up from inside the mud. Finally, he recognized what was happening and screamed for his sisters.

"The transformation is complete!" yelled Jamison. "He is Akuji Zār!"

In one motion, Arlo yanked his arms out of the mud and pointed at the hovering angels in the sky. The ground exploded, and thousands of skeletons shot out of the earth, sailing through the air toward Malaika and Haleena. The angels tried to outmaneuver the flying skeletons, but they were moving too fast. A skull with glowing eyes crashed into Haleena's head and bit off her ear before dozens more piled on her.

Malaika dodged several of the undead before punching a skeleton in its face, exploding its head. But hundreds were quickly on her. Malaika raised her hand, and a green light appeared in her fist.

"Stop this, Arlo!" she threatened, aiming her arm at the center of Arlo's chest.

Suddenly, a group of skeletons grabbed Malaika's arm, stopping her from aiming it at Arlo. One of the creatures bit the angel's forearm while another bent Malaika's arm until the palm full of energy was swinging around erratically. The zombies pulled her arm pulled in front of a group of skeletons, and Malaika released a ray of energy. A long, green light burst from her hand, exploding a group of creatures and spraying bone fragments everywhere. Malaika concentrated, keeping the electricity firing from her hand while allowing the undead to pull her arm erratically, hoping to destroy as many creatures as possible. Suddenly, a zombie with glowing red eyes and strips of leathery skin hanging from its skull rose from the mud. The monster didn't have legs and dragged its torso along the ground, moaning as its evil eyes focused on Malaika. As if awaiting instructions from its master, the creature looked at Arlo, waiting for his command. Arlo smiled at the beast. He could feel the zombie's desire to kill pulsating through his body, begging to kill the angel. This time, Arlo didn't need to throw mud. He could feel something inside, a feeling pushing him beyond the realm of the frail, lifeless boy clinging to a world that didn't want him. Arlo felt like the most powerful being in the world. The angels were nothing but insignificant flies to him. Arlo no longer needed to throw mud to push the zombies to do his bidding, nor did he need to tell them through the struggling communication of the words in his head. A thread connected him to all the dead in the universe, and he could pull those strings only by an inkling of intention. Arlo turned away from the zombie and tugged gently on the line of evil inside his body.

"ARGGGGG!"

As the zombie turned to face Malaika, an invisible force lifted it from the ground and hurled it toward the angel. As it flew through the air with the wind pulling its strands of gray hair back on its skull, the skin ripped away from its rotting meat and fell from the sky in shreds of dry strips. The zombie grabbed Malaika's arm, bit down hard, and bent Malaika's arm until the beam of light shot into her chest.

"Ahhhhhhh!" screamed Malaika.

Unable to turn off the electricity burning through her chest, Malaika started trembling, and a thick golden substance began pouring from her eyes.

"Malaika!" screamed Jamison.

Jamison climbed to his feet and pressed his hand against his chest, causing a golden light to radiate from inside his body. The bones attached to his back started glowing and flapping rapidly until tiny feathers appeared. Within seconds, the angel had new feathers on his back. With his feathers completely regenerated, Jamison shot into the sky. He shot a beam of light at the thousands of skeletons attacking his sisters but only hit a few. Realizing he was running out of time, Jamison lowered his head and closed his eyes.

"Father, please forgive me for what I am about to do."

Jamison opened his palm and fired a burst of energy into his face. As he closed his eyes and allowed the electricity to move through his body, thunder rumbled through the sky, and large pillowy clouds of iron-colored vapor appeared. Suddenly, the brown clouds exploded, continuously shooting brown lightning bolts into Jamison's chest. Jamison's skin turned as dark as the brown clouds, and his chest glowed. After a while, the lightning strikes stopped. Smoke billowed from Jamison's nose and mouth until the angel's body finally exploded, covering the sky in a brown mist that spread like chocolate fog. Suddenly, deep, powerful voices rang out inside the smoke.

"Cease your attack or face the wrath of Heaven's warriors!"

Arlo looked up and saw hundreds of glowing eyes filled with light staring at him from inside the brown mist. Soon, the fog cleared, and dozens of replicas of Jamison appeared in the sky. The copies of Jamison grabbed the skeletons, tore apart their frames, and threw their bones to the ground.

As bones rained from the sky, Arlo grew even angrier.

"I will have my revenge!" he yelled in a deep demonic voice.

Arlo suddenly began to levitate, and he turned away from the battle, drifting through the forest. As soon as he floated away from the angels, the carcasses of various dead animals rose from the earth, howling and screaming. Malaika saw her moment to escape and fired a burst of energy into the heads of the nearest zombies, exploding them and watching as the ash from their bones rained from the sky. More zombies rose from the earth and moved to defend Arlo as he moved further away into the forest.

"Don't let him get away!" yelled Malaika.

Suddenly, all the monsters turned on Malaika and shot into the air to attack her. The dozens of replicas of Jamison moved through the sky, shooting white light out of their palms, exploding the zombies. But more zombies rose from the mud, leaping upon the replicas. One of the zombies bit into one of the faux angel's necks, and the angel's eyes turned black before the angel's body exploded, sending sparks across the rainy sky. The other zombies took notice and started attacking all the replicas of Jamison like wild animals. Each of the copies of Jamison exploded one by one as the undead bit into their necks.

Coughing and wiping the dust from her eyes, Malaika blasted a trio of advancing skeletons before attempting to fly away. Just as she began descending, she heard her sister's voice.

"Malaika!" screamed Haleena. "Watch out!"

Just as Malaika was about to land, she looked down and saw the ground open up – a badly decomposed three-headed dog rose from the mud, opened its mouths, and tried biting the angel's foot off. Malaika flapped her wings and lifted herself from the monster's reach. As the beast snapped its jaws beneath her, Malaika moved her hand in a circular motion, and a glowing fire ring appeared. She clapped her hands together twice, and a ball of fire shot from the circle and landed on the demonic dog, exploding the ground and burning the creature to ash. This time, the carcasses of zombie animals rose from the earth shrieking. As soon as they saw Malaika, they leaped to attack, flying through the air.

Suddenly, one of the zombie animals froze and fell from the sky. Then another, and another. Soon, all the zombies' carcasses fell motionless to the ground; the only sound was the heavy rain falling on the leaves. Malaika flew over to Haleena and Jamison.

"What happened?" asked Malaika.

Jamison turned and looked in the direction he'd last seen Arlo.

"Arlo is going back to the city. The fight is beyond us now because he's too powerful. We must inform Father that Isadora's accidental removal from The Scrolls of Life has transformed Arlo into Akuji Zār – the God Zombie."

Haleena started crying, and drops of golden fluid dripped from her eyes.

"I didn't mean to do it. It was an accident."

Jamison turned to Haleena and wiped the tears from her face.

"Collect Isadora's remains and start the Ceremony of Reconciliation. Father told us there was no reversal, but I'll ask again. Maybe there's some way he can bring back Isadora's soul."

As Haleena and Malaika walked through the bones to Isadora's body, Jamison turned and looked into the rainy forest.

"So many will die at the hands of the Akuji Zār. I hope Father sends someone powerful to eliminate Arlo before it's too late."

8

Night of the Witch

"I've had it!"

Penny walked through the living room to the kitchen, where her sister Inez sprinkled seasoning into a boiling pot.

"The forest is crawling with those disgusting creatures. How much longer before we terminate the rain spell?"

Ignoring her sister, Inez grabbed an enormous lobster from the counter and dropped it in the pot. As the creature screamed, Inez opened the oven and checked on the baked potatoes.

"Shit. I should've made a bisque."

At that moment, their sister Indigo walked in, and Penny turned her frustration on her.

"Have you been out in that forest?"

Indigo ignored her sister and went to the boiling pot.

"Oh, you're making lobster tonight."

Indigo touched the boiling water with her index finger and shoved it into her mouth.

"Ummm.... Lobster's so good."

Angry that her sisters were ignoring her, Penny stepped in front of Indigo.

"Why are the two of you acting like bitches? I asked a question."

Indigo sighed and pulled her black hair into a ponytail. She quickly twirled her index finger, and a red scrunchy appeared; she calmly tucked her hair in place.

"Do we have to go through this every century? Jeez! I thought you would've learned the process by now. To answer your question, no. I haven't been outside today."

"Come with me."

Penny grabbed her sister by the arm and led her into the living room. She continued walking until the women passed through the energy wall and stood high above the forest.

"There!" said Penny.

Indigo looked down and saw chaos beneath them - hundreds of terrified people streaming through the forest, shrieking and crying, attempting to evade the demonic sounds coming from behind. Suddenly, their nightmares appeared; dozens of Huturo, some holding blood-covered heads attached to spinal cords, laughing like children at the terrified victims attempting to flee. As the group tried to escape, a hoard of vampires stumbled out of the darkness. Instead of eyes, the pail-skinned creatures had two suctioning mouths on their eye sockets and dozens of mouths on their bodies. The mouths sucked at the air, tasting it to locate their victims. The monsters immediately picked up on the scent of the Huturo and turned to attack them. But suddenly, they paused - the vampires could smell the fear of fleeing people and sprinted wildly after them. With a shriek, they ran into the crowd and attacked the men and children, pressing their suctioning bodies against them, draining their blood until the humans fell to the ground in ash.

While the vampires took their fill of victims, the Huturo moved through the crowd like an organized chainsaw, ripping off heads and stuffing their victims into their chests.

The two witches watched silently as a couple of Huturo zeroed in on two teenagers attempting to break away from the group. The boy and girl passed beneath the hovering witches and tried to outflank the monsters, but a naked vampire appeared, its body covered in dozens of sucking mouths. The girl was the closest, and the creature jumped on her, pulling the terrified girl close to its body. There came a popping sound, like numerous champagne bottles exploding - the vampire's mouths latched onto the girl's skin and began draining her blood.

"Jennifer!" screamed the boy.

The teenager pulled a gun from his pants and fired at the vampire, knocking it to the ground. Two Huturo ran toward him, and he got off another shot, hitting one of the creatures in the head before the other Huturo overpowered him and pulled his skull and spine out of his body. The Huturo's chest opened, and two wrinkled gray heads burst out, their black eyes glistening while they snarled and snapped their jaws. The Huturo grabbed the end of the boy's bloody spine and pushed it inside its body. The dead boy's eyes immediately opened, and he smiled sinisterly. He began hissing as the trio of evil skulls moved outside the body of the Huturo like snakes until the monster pushed them inside and its chest closed. With a high-pitched giggle, the creature's enormous eyes locked on a fresh victim and pursued.

After the hellacious scene moved away from the witches, a strange gas rose from the body of the dead Huturo, and strange vines began reaching out from their corpses, spreading along the ground and wrapping around the trees. Some of the vines shot into a cluster of bushes, and the foliage started shaking.

"Ah!" yelled a voice.

Penny and Indigo watched as a heavyset man emerged from his hiding spot. After looking around to make sure no monsters were present, he turned to walk in the opposite direction. The corpse of one of the Huturo lay in his path, spraying the strange mist along the ground. The man raised his foot to step over the monster and immediately regretted it – an orange liquid shot out of the corpse, covering the man's legs and genitals.

"AAAAHHH!" the man screamed, furiously wiping the front of his pants and legs.

Suddenly, the man stopped wiping his pants and looked at his hands – there were throbbing orange bumps all over them.

"Get it off!"

The man rubbed his hands furiously, trying to remove the dots, but more bubbles appeared, stretching his skin like taffy. With wide eyes, the terrified man held up his hands and watched as the bumps began popping, spraying his face with blood.

"Jesus! Lord help me!"

The man flipped his hands over and saw two enormous bumps stretching the skin on his palm until they, too, burst. As the fresh blood sprayed his face, the man didn't turn away – he saw dozens of tiny eyes staring at him from underneath the skin.

"W-w-what's that?" he asked.

Suddenly, the man screamed out in pain.

"Ahhhhhhhh!"

Both of his hands turned black and fell off his wrists like rotten pieces of meat. But instead of lying on the ground, the hands rose like giant spiders and scattered into the darkness. Unable to scream, the man started gagging.

"Gug... Gug...."

The terrified man lifted the nubs on his arms and stared at where his hands had been. As he stared at the shredded ends of his arms, he saw dozens of tiny teeth chewing from inside his skin.

"G-God, why is this...."

Suddenly, his body jerked, and he screamed.

"AAAAAHHH!"

A new pain made the man double over, and he tried reaching down to grab his genitals – but his hands were gone. A small stain appeared on the front of his pants and grew larger until it soaked him from the waist down.

"Gggggg..."

The man swiped his arm in front of his pants as if his hands were still attached but could not touch anything. Suddenly, a strange metallic sound rose in the night air - the creatures moving inside the man's pants chewed through the fabric, and a blanket of glowing worms emerged from the cloth covering his legs and torso like a blanket. Unable to escape his fate, the man fell to the ground, allowing the monstrous insects to feast on his body. Pink foam poured from his mouth as his eyes rolled in his head, and his chest shook as the worms chewed their way through his insides. Finally, with a great rush, the man's stomach rose like an enormous balloon and then collapsed. The bugs exploded out of his belly and covered his body, eating everything until nothing was left but brittle bones.

Penny and Indigo watched silently as the larvae, fat from eating human flesh, multiplied. The skeleton of the deceased cracked open, and a green mist emerged from inside his bones. As the smoke spread over the forest floor, the larvae began exploding, and tiny four-legged creatures emerged. The small slime-covered monsters grew to the size of a beetle but continued growing into something more sinister. As their bodies lay twisting and contorting on the ground, the monsters transformed into eyeless miniature dogs from Hell with gray hairless skin, howling and snapping their mouths in search of food. Soon, their gray skin began ripping, and tiny mouths appeared on their bodies. This appearance of the suctioning mouths made the creatures more aggressive, and they started attacking one another. Soon, hundreds of vampire dogs were everywhere, a whirlwind of chaos in the forest's center, howling with anger. When the last creature was at its final size, all the dogs raised their heads and bayed, filling the air with terrifying shrieks before running into the forest in one giant pack, searching for food.

Penny turned to her sister.

"There's no way you can tell me you're okay with this!"

Indigo sighed and turned away from the forest.

"It has to play out, Penny."

"Play out? These things are killing thousands, and millions will die before this ends. How long before Heaven discovers our part in all these deaths?"

"They didn't find out before."

"What? The Black Death? We never started that plague. That was different because we sat back and allowed nature to run its course."

"You need to get a hold of yourself. This new death isn't the only mass killing we've lived through. The Flu and the Smallpox - our finger-prints are on those mass deaths, too. It is the only way the clairvoyants can survive beyond the realms of Heaven, by redirecting souls that would otherwise go to Hell into the Orb of Jupiter."

Penny sucked her teeth and exhaled in frustration.

"We're no different than those fucking vampires."

"Don't say that, Penny. We are different. Those souls live in the Orb of Jupiter without pain, fortifying countless Clairvoyants with the energy to live. We don't torture them; they sleep peacefully, and the energy from their dreams helps us survive. After feeding the Clairvoyant Order for one hundred years, we release them to Heaven's intended destination – Hell."

"You don't need to explain to me how it works."

"I think I do. We go through this with you every one hundred years."

"But this situation is different, Indigo. We didn't cause or exacerbate those previous events. But we've taken a direct position against Heaven this time, and Hell is the beneficiary. It's one thing to sit back and use discarded souls to our benefit, but It's something completely different to help that bitch Asura. For years, she's been Hell's bitch, and the whole Clairvoyant Order knows it. But now she's tricked us into this mess. When Heaven comes for Asura, she'll have no problem pointing them in our direction, and she won't be wrong."

Indigo grabbed Penny's hand.

"Your head's swimming in nonsense. Come on, let's eat. You'll feel better once you've had some dinner and a good night's sleep."

Penny reluctantly allowed her sister to lead her back inside the house.

9

City Life

Arlo huddled in the bushes, watching the rainy streets in silence. The city he'd known for most of his life was gone, transformed into an alien wasteland filled with thick vines and weird plants. Eventually, Arlo spotted a familiar building. He stared at it, confused, unable to figure out where he'd seen it. Finally, it dawned on him that the structure used to be the shopping mall he visited after school with his friends; it was almost gone now, hidden beneath large glowing leaves that seemed to breathe in the rain, reaching out as if searching for something to eat.

Cars scattered in the middle of the street with the doors left ajar, some car alarms still singing eerie death songs. Arlo spotted several blood trails leading from a few cars into the street where a few headless bodies lay and knew what happened - the Huturo killed them and took their heads for trophies.

Arlo was about to move from the shadows into the street when his eyes fell on a corpse lying underneath a running vehicle. Although the body was headless, it was shaking, like the person was still alive, trying to pull itself out from under the car. The body shook a few more times before it exploded, sending larvae everywhere.

Arlo was expressionless as he stepped out from the bushes; he was not afraid of what he witnessed because he still felt the power to control the undead teaming in his body. As soon as he stepped onto the street, the whole world came alive; three Huturo, each holding a head with a spine attached, burst out of a nearby shop and sprinted toward him while a group of vampire dogs picked up on Arlo's scent and started running at him. Arlo calmly raised his hand, and suddenly the ground exploded in front of the attackers; a group of screaming skeletons with a green light illuminating their skulls emerged from the sewer. The mud-covered skeletons jumped on the creatures, biting into their necks and ripping out their veins, making them bleed out black blood until they fell.

As the zombies continued attacking the vicious vampire dogs and the Huturo, Arlo started walking up the stairs in front of the mall. Just as he reached the top, he paused – something was standing at the entrance, a silver mist in the rain resembling a silhouette. It appeared, faded away, and reappeared like a shadow in fog. Arlo stared at the strange shape, unsure of what he was seeing. Was it the angels trying a new line of attack? Was it a new creature from hell coming to claim its place in his world? Arlo allowed the energy coursing through his body to take over. He effortlessly pushed the power out through his arms and feet and pulled it all back in like a magnet. Soon, the ground all around started rumbling. As he watched the silvery shadow dancing in front of the mall entrance, spindly arms exploded out of the earth. Soon, the entire road buckled as the corpses of the dead animals and humans pushed through the asphalt, screaming and moaning in agony as they moved toward their master. But Arlo didn't stop calling out to his army. If heaven sent this new creature, he knew he'd be battling something deadlier than the angels. Arlo rose in the air and pushed into the ground beneath his feet. Arlo could feel the movement of creatures beneath him and called upon them to assist. But he didn't stop there. Arlo also summoned the undead hiding in the forest behind them. Although the vampires destroyed most creatures, he called upon the remaining zombies to do his bidding. Within seconds, the growling undead tore through the trees and sprinted toward Arlo.

With his horrific Army standing behind him, Arlo stood at the entrance to the mall, waiting for the creature to attack.

But nothing happened.

Frustrated, Arlo moved toward the shimmering creature, daring it to show aggression. But Arlo's movements didn't affect the shadow; it drifted in and out of sight, seemingly trying to form a cohesive shape. Arlo moved closer and squinted, trying to see the creature's face. Suddenly, an icy whisper echoed in the air.

"Arrrrrrrloooooo."

Arlo froze in his tracks. Although the noise from the army of zombies rose like a thunderous mob, the whisper penetrated his soul with the accuracy of a laser, making him feel something he hadn't felt since he died – fear.

"Arrrrrrloooo," the voice cried out again.

"W-w-who are you?" asked Arlo.

Arlo felt confused. For the first time, he felt a duality in his existence; anger weighed on him like an oversized hat, pushing him to destroy everything in his sight. But there was also Arlo the teenager - a young kid fond of poetry and playing video games with his friend. Yes, there were two entities in his body, and for some reason, the silver silhouette was bringing everything to the surface, making Arlo want to cry. For the first time, he took pity on his predicament. Arlo felt out of place in this world of rot and stench, like a joker in a deck of cards; part of the game, but so strange and different that he questioned why he existed. Arlo felt like running away and leaving the world behind. As he watched the mist, Arlo felt his emotions moving further away from the world of war and, instead, moving closer to his true identity.

"Maybe I'm dreaming," whispered Arlo.

Arlo closed his eyes and took a deep breath - he could smell the fresh sheets on his bed at home, the soft lips of his mother's kiss as she coaxed him to wake up. Arlo could almost hear the alarm clock going off on his nightstand.

When Arlo opened his eyes, the shadow was hovering before the side of the building. This time, Arlo could see an image – a blonde-haired woman with no face floating above the ground like a sheet in the wind. Arlo rubbed his eyes, but he still couldn't see her face.

"Arrrrrrloooooo," the voice called again.

Soon, the ghostly image pushed through the walls and disappeared. After watching for a few moments, Arlo followed.

10

Closing In

Asura emerged from the forest and looked around before motioning to the bushes.

"Come on," she whispered.

John walked out of the forest, and Claire followed.

"How are you feeling, Asura?" asked John. "Have you recovered from the injuries you sustained in our communication with Lord Balam?"

Asura reached underneath her robe and pulled out her blood-covered hand.

"The healing spell is working fine. Don't worry."

John winced as he pressed his palm against his chest.

"The spell you cast is working, but Lord Balam was more brutal to me. My burns haven't healed yet."

Claire stumbled out of the woods and walked up behind John and Asura.

"Why have we stopped?" asked Claire, ignoring their conversation.

Asura sneered at Claire.

"She's such a pain in the ass. Please, Master. Let me kill her so we can eliminate her infernal stupidity," said Asura.

Claire rolled her eyes and spoke to John.

"I don't want to be here with either of you. Manuel, where is my son?"

"My name is John now, Mrs. Ortega."

Claire sighed in frustration.

"Okay, *John*. Where's Arlo? Is he here?"

John pointed toward the mall.

"He's inside."

Claire was about to walk across the street when she spotted the corpses of several vampire dogs and Huturo lying on the ground. She moved closer to John and stood watching the strange mist rising from the corpse of the Huturo.

"How do we get inside?"

John turned to Asura.

"Are you strong enough to give us protection?"

"I am."

John turned to Claire.

"Mrs. Ortega, you're going to have to stay close now. If you don't, we can't protect you."

Asura opened her palm, and a green ball of electricity rose from her hand. The ball continued growing until it encircled the trio in a protective forcefield. The trio walked across the street and was about to enter the building when a pack of vampire dogs attacked. When the creatures touched the forcefield, they cried in pain and backed away. Asura, John, and Claire moved into the building.

11

New Evil

Arlo sat on the floor and looked up at the ceiling. The mall's roof was gone, destroyed by an enormous alien tree that had grown from several levels beneath his position. Arlo couldn't take his eyes off the plant; its appearance seemed like something out of a nightmare; the black leaves were thick and spongey and leaked a red fluid that appeared to be blood. There were no insects, yet the tree made sounds like cicadas. Its bark was see-thru, like glass, revealing something more sinister inside – human heads with twisted, painful expressions on their pale faces floating in a thick liquid. The tree creaked and shuddered as the faces moved inside, their cries silenced by the thick mucus that smothered them all. Finally, disgusted by the sight of the plant from hell, Arlo turned away.

Arlo looked around the mall, searching for the shadowy figure he'd seen enter the building. He'd tried following the ghost, but as soon as Arlo entered the building, the figure disappeared, and he could not find it again. As Arlo sat on the floor waiting for the shadowy figure to re-emerge, the teenager couldn't help but wonder if the hoard of zombies behind him was scaring it. Arlo reached inside himself with his mind and tugged on the strings of power he used to control the zombies; suddenly, the zombies that were closest to him moved back.

Suddenly, Arlo heard a noise. He turned to see a teenager pull down the cage of a shoe store, lock it with keys, and run into the back. The other zombies saw the boy, too, and several ran to the cage to attack, but Arlo used his power to hold them back. It had been so long since Arlo ate, and the sweet, freezing taste of the teenager's brains belonged to him.

"Go ahead. Kill the boy," a voice whispered in Arlo's head.

Arlo sprinted to the store and waved his hand in front of the wired frame; the metal peeled back like an orange peel, and Arlo shot inside. He hadn't realized it before, but he was hungry; thick green saliva was dripping from his jowls, and a wheezing sound was coming from his throat. It had been so long since he fed, and although he couldn't feel the fires of Sun Oil consuming his body, he knew it was only a matter of time before the flames engulfed him, punishing him for not devouring the forbidden delicacy of brain matter.

The store was dark, and there was barely any light, but Arlo knew where the boy was hiding; he was in the storage closet near the stack of tennis rackets, betrayed by the smell of fear in the air and the beating of his terrified heart.

Thump-thump. Thump-thump.

The beating heart told Arlo everything about his victim; he knew the teenager's height, whether he would run or if the teenager wanted to defend himself. Arlo felt the boy's heart was talking to him, transmitting everything Arlo needed to know before he accosted his victim and ripped him apart.

Arlo calmly walked through the piles of merchandise scattered on the floor and stood at the stockroom door. Although hungry, Arlo took the time to breathe in the victim's fear, to smell his insides. Arlo took a deep breath and felt cold liquid dripping down his legs; it was bloody urine. Arlo was so excited to kill the boy and taste his brains that he'd lost all control of his body. The smell of the boy's fear was enthralling. It touched parts of Arlo that he didn't realize existed. It filled him with the desire to kill, to murder, to take in all his victim's internal organs like a warm dinner, to partake of his deepest secrets, to invade all parts of the boy and overcome every aspect of his body like an enormous wave of evil. Arlo's stomach made strange noises now, filling the air with gurgling sounds as the liquid in his belly prepared to take in what was his to have. He longed to see his victim's life drift away as he ripped apart his skull, that faraway look in his eyes, the last bit of fight before the ocean of death pulled him under.

Arlo waved his hand in front of the door, and a mighty wind sucked the door inward, splintering it and sending shredded wood raining down on the scared boy.

"God! No!" screamed the terrified boy, covering his head.

Arlo immediately went to the boy and grabbed the child's wrists, twisting them until he heard the bones crack.

"Ahhhhh!"

Thump-thump-thump. Thump-thump-thump.

Arlo jumped on the boy and bit his forehead. Blood sprayed all over the room, and the child screamed louder.

"Ahhhh! Mommy!"

But Arlo was too deep in his evil deeds to hear the bloody cries. His mouth filled with sweet, iron-filled blood, bone, and hair. Arlo sucked up the blood like a vacuum, trying his best not to let a drop escape his mouth. Soon, the boy's body went limp, and the crying ceased - this turned Arlo on more, and he lost all control and ripped off the top of the boy's skull with such force that blood started pouring out of the catatonic teen's nose. The top of his victim's head fell to the floor, and Arlo was immediately on all fours to retrieve it, careful not to waste a single morsel of brain matter. After recovering the top of the head, Arlo used his bottom teeth to scrape the cranium bone clean of blood, vessels, and goop. Arlo closed his eyes in delight as the sweet taste of brains cooled his body like peppermint. After licking the top of the skull clean, Arlo turned his attention to the top of the teenager's head. Finally, what he wanted most was his for the taking – brains. Arlo pressed his lips gently onto the gelatin substance and moaned – it was sweeter than the last time he took a life. Arlo bit into the matter, and that freezing feeling intensified, making him feel high, wiping away the remnants of hunger like a painkiller. Arlo ate his fill until the boy's skull was empty, and the body tumbled on its side. Feeling satisfied, Arlo stumbled back and stared at the corpse; he was shocked to realize in addition to consuming his victim's brain, Arlo had also eaten the boy's eyeballs and half his forehead.

Arlo wiped his mouth and looked around before walking out of the store into the shopping mall. He made his way back over to the weird tree and sat down on the ground.

"Where are you?" whispered Arlo as he searched for the ghostly figure.

"I'm here," a voice responded.

Arlo turned and saw a ghostly silhouette floating beside him. He immediately used his powers to fly into the air, levitating above the silvery shadow as he looked down.

"Show yourself before I call the zombies to attack."

The shadow continued floating in place, unfazed by the threat.

Arlo pushed gently on the power inside his body, and a group of undead came rushing from behind. They saw the shadow and leaped forward to attack but passed through the shadow and crashed into the strange tree. The tree automatically reacted to the presence of the zombies, and a deep gash appeared in the trunk. Suddenly, a hand made of gelatin liquid shot out of the opening and grabbed the undead, pulling them inside with the other dead skulls. Trapped, the zombies thrashed back and forth inside the muck, trying to free themselves, but they could not escape. There was an explosion inside the liquid, and bubbles surrounded everything. Suddenly, the eyes of the skulls lit up, and the monsters started screaming, menacing grimaces on their faces. The zombies thrashed about, trying to move away from the heads, but their resistance couldn't save them; the skulls began feasting on their bodies, biting into their flailing arms and tearing them off their bodies. As black blood colored the clear liquid, the zombie blood seemed to make the skulls more aggressive, and they bit into the stomachs of the undead, tearing their intestines out and shredding them with their teeth like voracious piranha. The skull demons continued biting on the bodies of their victims until the tree trunk became black, pieces of skin and appendages appearing and disappearing in the cloud of liquid. In contrast, the eerie light of the skulls lit up the tree like nightlights from hell.

Finally, all the light disappeared, and the tree started swaying back and forth. Once again, the sound of cicadas echoed in the mall. After a few seconds, the darkness in the liquid melted away, and the tree trunk was clear again – a fresh batch of heads trapped within, all opening and closing their mouths, twisting their faces in excruciating expressions of pain.

After witnessing the demise of the zombies, Arlo gathered his power and sent out a message with his mind to the hoard of zombies waiting in the shadows behind him.

"Stay away until I call you. The tree is dangerous."

Arlo turned his attention back to the silver shadow.

"Why are you following me?"

The shadow disappeared and then reappeared.

"I'm here to help you," replied a tiny voice.

"Help me? With what?"

"To kill the world."

The voice seemed familiar, and Arlo moved closer, trying to see the ghost's face.

"I know you," whispered Arlo.

"Yes," the voice replied. "You do."

Arlo's eyes began to water.

"Say it," whispered the voice.

Arlo's voice was thick with tears.

"I-Isadora? Is that you?"

"I think so, but I don't know for sure."

The words hit Arlo like a ton of bricks. Without realizing it, he sobbed, happy to have his companion back in this world of pure hell.

"I can't believe it's you! But how?"

The shadow took the form of a large red sphere before turning pink and transforming into the silhouette of a man with horns atop his head. Next, the shadow transformed into the shape of a large growling dog before changing once more into the form of a girl.

"I think it's me, but I'm not sure."

"What do you mean?"

"I feel the same, but I'm different. It's hard for me to focus for longer than a few seconds."

Confused, Arlo tried remembering the things he liked about Isadora.

"I remember the way you looked. You had short hair and were a bit of a tomboy, but you had these brilliant brown eyes that shined like diamonds. Don't you remember?"

"No. Whenever I try to remember the person I was, my mind is overwhelmed with rage."

Arlo ran his fingers through the pink mist.

"And me. You remember me, don't you?"

The pink fog wrapped itself around Arlo like a rope of smoke.

"What I remember most is what the angels took from me."

Arlo also remembered what the angels had taken. He remembered the moments he and Isadora spent in the Priming Fields and how they'd professed their love for one another. But soon, his mind flashed moments of Isadora screaming, falling to the ground with her guts spilling out. He remembered the rage, how lonely he'd felt as her life lay extinguished in the rain. That moment felt like a nightmare, a horrible reminder of Heaven's evil towards them. But now Isadora was here fighting for the love Heaven tried to take away. Somehow, she'd clawed back from the brink of nothingness, fighting to be by his side again.

"I want to see you, Isadora."

The fog began shimmering like diamonds as the smoke drifted around Arlo's waist and chest before forming a pink halo around the crown of his head.

"I've tried to recreate the image of who I once was, but I can't. My mind's like mush, filled with evil thoughts. The only time I'm at peace is when I empty my mind."

"You have to try."

The pink smoke unwrapped itself from Arlo's body and gathered before him. Soon, Arlo saw the silhouette of a woman.

"It's working," whispered Arlo. "You've almost got it."

A face flashed amongst the pink clouds, and Arlo smiled – it was Isadora's.

"I saw your face! You're almost here!"

The pink clouds became gray, and lightning bolts flashed inside the shadow. A clap of thunder rang out in the mall, and a figure appeared – a naked woman with a giant hole in the center of her chest and thousands of worms pouring out of the wound. Isadora's face was there, but half of her face started melting like wax.

"Argh," she cried, choking as her melted flesh dripped inside her mouth.

Arlo was terrified.

"Focus, Isadora!"

Isadora's face stopped melting, and she covered her face with both palms. Suddenly, the thousands of worms froze in her chest, and they all tumbled to her feet, landing on the floor and shattering into ice crystals. Arlo watched in astonishment as the hole in the center of Isadora's chest began shrinking until only her naked gray breasts appeared. Meanwhile, a strange blue light started burning beneath her palms, and the melted flesh dripping from her chin began climbing up Isadora's fingers and disappeared beneath her covered face.

Arlo was excited.

"You did it!"

Arlo grabbed Isadora's arms and pulled her hands down from her face. As soon as he did, he jumped back in fear – Isadora had a disfigured face; the skin that melted from her face hadn't returned but froze, and the icy gray skin hung from her skull like a frozen waterfall. The other part of her face was drooping; the icy skin on the other side pulled on the other half, making her eyes, nose, and lips seem askew. Isadora's eyes were intact but red like hot coals in a fire, revealing something sinister within.

Isadora jumped on Arlo, knocking him to the ground.

"We will kill them all!"

Arlo tried pushing Isadora aside, but she was too strong. She held him in place and moved her face close to his.

"I've missed you. Did you miss me?"

Arlo couldn't speak. He didn't recognize the evil spirit holding him down.

"G-get off me!" he stammered. "You're not Isadora!"

"You love me, and I love you! Can't you see? We're eternally connected."

"Get the fuck off me!" yelled Arlo.

Suddenly, Arlo remembered his zombie army and called out to him with his mind:

"Come! Get her off me!"

The zombies poured out of the darkness in hundreds, rushing to Arlo's position to save him from Isadora. A skeleton and a one-armed man were the first to reach them, and they sailed through the air to attack Isadora. But the disfigured girl remained in place, holding Arlo down without glancing in their direction. The zombies passed through the girl's body like she was air, unable to remove her from atop Arlo.

"Can't you see, Arlo? I'm here because of you. Nothing else can harm me."

Arlo called out for more undead to attack, but they all passed through the woman like a shadow, unable to touch her.

"Your heart belongs to me."

Isadora looked down at the gaping wound in Arlo's side and stuck her hand inside, making Arlo jump; he could feel her icy touch moving inside his dead organs, sliding up towards his chest. When Isadora's hand reached his heart, Arlo opened his mouth in surprise – Isadora's touch sent a shockwave of coldness through him like a thousand needles.

"No! P-p-please! S-s-so cold!"

Isadora moved her disfigured face close to Arlo and kissed his lips. Suddenly, he felt something inside his body tear. He felt Isadora's hand quickly slither out of the opening in his side. She rose to stand above Arlo and held her hand before him – Isadora held his blackened heart in her hand!

"Can't you see, Arlo? You are mine, and I am yours!"

Isadora opened her twisted mouth and shoved the rotting piece of tissue inside. As she chewed, thick black liquid squirted from her mouth, splashing down Arlo's face.

"You!" yelled Arlo while climbing to his feet. "What the hell are you?"

As Isadora chewed Arlo's heart, she stared back at him with red eyes while he stared at her, emotionless, combing through his feelings. For reasons he couldn't understand, seeing Isadora eat his heart made him fear her – and crave her companionship. Arlo started seeing the situation for what it was. They were two lost souls fighting against everything and everyone: Heaven and Hell, the decomposition of their flesh, and the never-ending pursuit of the grave to snatch away their existence.

Arlo watched Isadora eating pieces of his body and didn't turn away. Now he could see the power of their connection; Isadora's murder at the hands of the angels brought them closer, connecting them through all eternity. He needed Isadora, and she needed him – to go on.

Still, there were so many questions Arlo had: Was Isadora a ghost or a monster? Who or what made her this way? If they remained together, where could they go to find peace? Would they constantly be hounded by two warring factions intent on inflicting their rule over a blind world?

Isadora swallowed the last mouthful of meat and moved closer to Arlo.

"I don't know."

"What?"

"I don't know how I survived or where we're going."

"Me either."

"They lied to us, Arlo. They tried to take away our love. Heaven is just as evil as Hell."

Arlo shook his head in agreement.

"What do you want me to do, Isadora?"

"Let's kill them all."

"Who?"

"Anyone that gets in our way."

"There's nowhere for us to go."

"It doesn't matter. As long as we're together."

Arlo reached out and grabbed Isadora's breast – it was as cold as ice. He closed his eyes and kissed her disfigured face. As he did, he tore off one of her breasts and dropped it to the ground. Isadora closed her eyes and continued kissing Arlo.

"Go ahead. Take it," whispered Isadora.

Arlo stuck his tongue into Isadora's mouth. The stench of rotting flesh enveloped him. Still, he was happy to have someone with him, to not be lonely in a world of monsters. Heaven and Hell had tested their love, and they survived - nothing could tear them apart. Slowly, Arlo pushed his hand through the wound on Isadora's chest. She barely moved as he ripped open her sternum, and cracking bones echoed in the mall. Arlo pushed through her organs, grabbed her heart, and pulled it from her chest. He gave Isadora another kiss, this time with his eyes open. While staring into her eyes, he put her heart into his mouth and ate it.

12

Mother's Milk

John, Asura, and Claire huddled behind a water fountain, watching Arlo pace back and forth. There were dozens of zombies behind him, growling and snarling, awaiting his command, but Arlo seemed oblivious to them; he was watching a strange tree that had broken the roof. Arlo's transformation slightly amused John; he no longer resembled the quiet boy who always looked one step behind the world. Arlo was a product of evil now, taking lives when Arlo deemed it necessary while disregarding the Sunday School bullshit their parents had tried shoving down their throats. John found it funny that although they took different paths, he and his best friend Arlo were central figures in the new evil world.

"Is it him?" whispered Claire nervously. "Is that my Arlo?"

Asura sighed and turned to John.

"Can we just kill her, Master?" she whispered, frustrated. "She's an eternal pain in the ass."

John shook his head in disagreement before turning to Claire.

"Yes, that's Arlo, Mrs. Ortega, but you need to be quiet. Arlo isn't the same boy we knew; if he hears us, all those monsters will attack."

Claire's eyes lit up.

"Arlo! My son!"

Claire stood and was preparing to run when John reached out and touched her arm.

"Arrrrrrr...."

Claire's body froze before she could step, and she fell to the ground. As Claire lay on the floor, her mouth opened and closed like a fish gasping for air, her wide eyes looking all around as she lay unable to move.

John leaned over her and whispered in her ear.

"I'm sorry, Mrs. Ortega, but I tried to warn you to be quiet."

As John continued watching Arlo, Asura leaned over Claire and whispered.

"If it were up to me, I'd cut your eyes out and send you into the storm like the senseless fool you are."

Suddenly, John moved to the other side of the fountain, leaving Asura alone with Claire. As he watched Arlo enter the clothing store, Asura continued speaking to Arlo's mother.

"Try holding your breath when the Huturo and the Vampires catch wind of your scent. Maybe they'll take you for dead and walk past, but I'm hoping they find out you're alive. Nothing would please me more than seeing them feast on your guts."

Asura ran to John's side and left Claire lying catatonic on the floor.

"Where did he go?" asked Asura.

"He's inside the shop," replied John.

The two watched Arlo emerge from the shop, covered in fresh blood. He walked over to the tree and began talking – to no one.

"Who is he talking to?" asked John.

Asura was unable to see anyone. Suddenly, an invisible force knocked Arlo to the ground.

"Is this an attack from the Angels?" asked John.

"Wait a minute," replied Asura.

Asura reached into her robe and retrieved a tiny leather bag. She stuck her index finger inside and covered it in black sparkling sand.

"Le-vei no-kelu!"

The old woman closed her eyes and rubbed the sand on her eyelid. When she opened her eyes, she smiled wickedly.

"What is it?" asked John. "What do you see?"

"Death," replied Asura. "Arlo is alone."

"What do you mean?"

"The girl Isadora is a spirit now."

"But how is that possible? Wasn't she a zombie just like Arlo?"

"She was, but something must've happened."

John watched as Arlo called the army of zombies to attack his position.

"Master, if we're going to engage Arlo, now would be the best time. He's alone and vulnerable."

"You stay here and keep an eye on Mrs. Ortega. If Arlo attacks, we'll need to use her to escape."

John raised himself from the floor and crept closer to Arlo. He watched as the invisible force reached inside Arlo's stomach and pulled out his heart. As his friend squirmed on the floor, John saw the rotting piece of meat hover in the air before something started biting chunks out of it. Soon, Arlo rose from the ground and started talking. After a few minutes, he began kissing the air. Arlo reached for something, and suddenly, he was holding a black heart. As soon as Arlo started consuming the flesh, John saw his opportunity and stepped out from the shadows.

13

Remembering a Friendship

"Sometimes...."

Startled by the word, Arlo turned around and looked at the shadowy figure beside the fountain.

"Sometimes," continued John. "I think about my best friend."

Arlo watched silently as his best friend moved closer.

"What's the matter, Arlo? Don't you remember me?"

Arlo remained silent, watching and listening. Meanwhile, the invisible Isadora leaned over and wrapped her pale arms around Arlo's waist while watching the approaching teenager. Although her lips didn't move, she spoke in Arlo's head just as she'd done before she died.

"I know him," she whispered. *"It's Manuel."*

As John continued inching closer, he opened his arms in a display of vulnerability.

"I'm not here to hurt you. I only want to talk."

Arlo felt Isadora's icy fingertips rubbing the back of his neck. Although she wasn't speaking to him directly, her words echoed in his mind, informing him, reminding him.

"He's not your friend anymore. His name is John now."

Finally, Arlo spoke.

"Fuck you, *ton of a bish,*"

Arlo had meant to call his friend a *son of a bitch*, but suddenly, he realized both his front teeth were gone – destroyed when he bit into his victim's skull.

"You're angry. I know," replied John. "A lot has happened since we last saw one another."

Suddenly, the night in the cavern was fresh in Arlo's mind; he could see the thousands of worms eating his flesh as he emerged from the underground lake and the cries of the tortured prisoners in their cages. Arlo remembered the smell of rotten flesh thick in the caverns, burning his nostrils like ammonia as he and Manuel moved through the darkness. Arlo could see it all now; he remembered watching as the towering monster that was the original John killed and tortured his prisoners before their eyes. Arlo remembered the cold steal as his hand fell on a weapon, the way he grabbed it and prepared to attack, the sharp pain shooting into his brain as his best friend plunged the knife into his back, the feeling of being pulled into darkness as he turned to look at Manuel in shock, betrayed by the friend who always promised to have his back.

"You can't trust him. He has a secret. I can see it on his face," whispered Isadora.

Arlo called out to his zombie army.

"Kill that fucker!"

The zombies roared as they sprinted out of the darkness toward John. As they attacked, Asura stepped out from her hiding spot and lifted her palm – the forcefield that protected them earlier reappeared, and the monsters crashed into it. As soon as the zombies touched the blue ball of energy, they crashed to the floor, frozen with faraway looks on their disfigured faces.

"I know you're mad, but if you put your anger aside, we may be able to help one another," yelled John.

The words infuriated Arlo, and he hissed in anger. He pointed at the floor beneath John's feet, and suddenly the entire building trembled.

"Master!" yelled Asura. "Run!"

Just as John tried to run, the floor exploded only a few feet before him – something was pushing from underneath the pile of zombies. As he watched the rise and fall of the bodies, John moved away, preparing himself for what was trying to get out. Suddenly, an explosion ripped apart the corpses, sending body parts flying in all directions.

"Master!" screamed Asura.

John stumbled back, still protected by the electric bubble, trying to regain his balance. There was an enormous hole in the floor where the zombies had been. Cautiously, John peered over the edge to see two vast glowing red eyes staring at him. He immediately backed away.

"Asura!" yelled John. "Get the woman!"

As Asura dashed to obey John's commands, a loud noise sounded from inside the hole.

CLICK-CLACK! CLICK-CLACK!

CLICK-CLACK! CLICK-CLACK!

Suddenly, a colossal skull emerged from the hole – the skeleton of a giant snake with large fangs.

"Holy shit!" exclaimed Asura.

The creature was so large that it seemed like a giant from a prehistoric era. There was no skin or blood on bones covered in sewage. The beast skidded along the damaged floor, its bones scratching the ground like fingernails on a chalkboard. It lifted itself and roared at John, preparing to attack.

"Asura! Where is the woman?" yelled John.

Asura ran over to Claire and placed her index finger on the woman's head. Claire immediately started blinking.

"W-where am I?" asked Claire, her cloudy eyes looking around.

Asura grabbed a handful of Claire's hair and pulled the woman to her feet.

"Get off your ass, bitch! Time to earn your pay!"

As Asura dragged Claire close to the activity, the skeleton snake bit into the energy ball that protected John. There was a loud popping sound, and the smell of metal was in the air, but the snake was unfazed -

unlike the zombies, the electricity didn't affect the skeleton and seemed to make the creature angrier. It raised itself high in the air and used gravity to penetrate the bubble with a powerful bite, but it couldn't get inside. When it didn't work, it bit again and again. Bolts of electricity were flashing everywhere, but the creature continued attacking. John's protective shield dimmed, blinking intermittently until it finally de-activated, leaving the teenager open for the snake's attack. The snake attacked and bit into John's chest with its large fangs.

John stumbled back and grabbed the creature's head as it dug its fangs deep into the boy's body. Wincing, John pulled the head of the monster from his body. Blood started to shoot from the open wound on John's chest, but he concentrated on the snake. John tore the monster's head from its body with one powerful movement. Although the serpent was headless, the snake's body thrashed wildly, crashing into windows and turning shops into piles of rubble. John held the red-eyed beast in his clutches as it snapped at him angrily. While the creature continued attacking, John turned to face Arlo.

"I possess the power of all those that came before me," John growled as he struggled to contain the beast.

John tried to destroy the monster by sticking his hand inside the serpent's mouth to pry apart its head, but he miscalculated, and the creature's arm-length fang bit through John's hand.

John smiled at Arlo.

"Lord Balam prepared me for this moment," exclaimed John while smiling. "I feel no pain."

John quickly freed himself and ripped off the creature's blood-covered fangs. He grabbed the top of the monster's mouth with one hand, and with the other, he held its lower jaw. With one powerful thrust, he pulled the monster's head apart. The creature's bottom jaw crashed to the floor and shattered into numerous pieces while John lifted the remaining part of the skull and stared at its glowing eyes. Although the beast lost its fangs and didn't have a bottom jaw, it con-tinued moving its upper jaw in a fruitless attempt to attack the teenager.

John threw the skull at Arlo, and it crashed on the floor. Still smiling with an enormous hole in his stomach, John covered the wound with his palm.

"No matter what this world does to us, we're still friends," said John.

John's words angered Arlo even more, and he prepared to attack his best friend again. Arlo closed his eyes and concentrated, reaching deep within the soil in search of zombies to do his bidding. Like thousands of fingers made of energy, Arlo clawed through rock and sediment with his invisible energy until he found hundreds of skeletons buried in the dirt beneath the building. He both pushed and pulled with energy until the eyes of the dead opened, glowing with the red energy that Arlo gave them. The ground rumbled as the zombies clawed through the dirt to defend their master.

As Arlo waited for his army to attack, Isadora wrapped her loving arms around his waist, her disfigured face drooping as she moved close to her boyfriend; Isadora was happy to be by his side again, ready to fight anything threatening their love. Although a hole remained in the center of her translucent body, she glowed with love. Being by Arlo's side while they fought against the world was where she wanted to be.

"Do it, my love. Kill him!" she whispered in Arlo's ear.

Shards of glass and rock chunks rained from above as the entire mall began shaking. Soon, dozens of decaying hands and skeletal appendages tore apart the floor as moans echoed in the mall.

"Uhhhhhh..."

An enormous explosion shot debris everywhere, and Arlo smiled as he watched his zombies climb out of the ground, some with decaying flesh while others were only skeletons, all heeding his call. The creatures looked at their master before facing their target – John. As they sprinted across the mall to fulfill the God Zombie's demand, John remained in place, a strange, eerie smile on his face. Arlo watched as his friend turned and nodded at something hidden in the darkness.

"Arlo!" yelled a voice from the shadows.

Arlo ignored the cry and continued pushing his zombies to kill John.

"Arlo, please! Stop!"

Suddenly, Asura stepped out from the shadows, dragging something along the floor toward John – it was Claire, Arlo's mother!

Arlo watched in disbelief as Asura lifted his mother from the ground by her hair.

"Ow! Let go of me, you bitch!"

Claire swung angrily at Asura, but the witch dodged the blows and slapped Claire's face while maintaining a firm grip on her hair.

"Call them off!" the witch yelled to Arlo.

Arlo couldn't believe what he was witnessing. He thought his mom was dead.

"M-mom?" asked Arlo, his voice thick with death. "I-I thought you were dead."

Arlo's emotions were all over the place; he missed his mom and was so grateful that she was alive, but he was also confused and afraid. Why had hell spared his mother and taken his father? Why was John holding his mother captive? Arlo remembered how his friend had betrayed him and knew it was only a matter of time before John killed his mother.

Arlo struggled with his thoughts, trying to understand what was happening. But he forgot about the zombie army he'd summoned. He didn't realize he'd placed his mother in harm's way until the first group of zombies launched themselves at John. Just as the monsters reached out to grab the boy, Asura held up her free arm and shot a fistful of white light at her master. The light hit John in the small of his back, and he fell to the ground while the zombies flew over him. Asura's hand lit up once more, and she fired again. This time, the light enveloped John in a ball of light, and the remaining zombies crashed into it, screaming as the electricity burned them, causing an enormous fireball.

"Call them off!" yelled Asura.

The floor exploded next to Claire, and one of the zombies bit into her ankle.

"AHHHHH!" she screamed as the teeth sunk into her flesh.

Asura jerked Claire out of the way, but her leg was still in the zombie's mouth. Asura let go of Claire's hair and pulled the monster off Claire's leg.

"Ow!" screamed Claire.

Asura quickly ripped the zombie's arms off and slammed it on the ground. Another monster jumped on Asura's back and bit into her neck. Claire saw her opportunity to escape and tried to run away. She had only taken a few steps when Asura slammed the zombie to the ground, tore off its head, grabbed the rotting corpse, and threw it at Arlo's mom. The headless body slammed into Claire's legs, latching on, causing her to fall to the floor on her face. The torso of the creature straddled the back of Claire's legs. As if forgetting its missing skull, it slammed its chest onto the woman's thighs and buttocks, attempting to bite her with a head it no longer possessed. It started climbing up her body, leaking black goo all over her neck and head. Asura walked over and pulled the zombie off Arlo's mother.

"That'll teach your dumb ass," the old lady barked, flinging the zombie into the wall. Asura grabbed Claire by her hair again and slammed her face to the ground to daze her.

"Hey, boy!" yelled Asura to Arlo. "Look at me!"

Asura held up her fist, and it exploded in flame.

"A hard head makes a soft ass!" Asura hissed.

The witch put her burning hand on Claire's head, and it burst into flame.

"AHHHHH!" screamed Claire.

Asura held the woman in place, delighted by the sounds of Claire's screams. The witch breathed deep as the smoke rose from Arlo's mother's scalp.

"Ahhhh! It burns! It burns!" cried Claire.

"Oh, shut your trap. Everyone loves barbecue," teased Asura.

The witch allowed the fire to continue burning until she saw blisters on Claire's scalp. Finally, she quickly opened and closed her hand, and the fire on Claire's scalp disappeared. Claire sank to the ground with her scalp sizzling and blisters covering half her head.

"You bitch!" cried Claire, clutching her head in pain.

"Mom!" yelled Arlo.

"Call off your zombies, or I'll tear this bitch to pieces!"

Arlo closed his eyes and sent out a message to the zombies.

"Stop!" he yelled inside his head.

The remaining zombies stopped advancing and lowered themselves to the floor, waiting on their master's command.

John moved closer to Arlo until he was standing in front of him.

"Now that we've gotten that out of the way, I have a proposition for you."

14

Send Me

Penny was trying to fall asleep as she always did - hovering only a few inches above her bed with two coins on her eyelids, her naked body covered in ice crystals. It was a trick she'd learned many years ago from a sorceress in Angola; the ice crystals, made from a cup of frozen tap water, regulated her body temperature and prevented the magical energy flowing within her body from waking her during sleep. Usually, Penny would be sleeping now, traversing alien planets or creating new spells in her room of isolation hidden beneath the ocean. But something kept her trapped in this dimension, a rumbling sound pulling her back each time she went inside herself. It was the sound of her two sisters' snoring.

"Freaking pigs," whispered Penny.

Penny lifted her pinky and shot out a burst of energy. The small ball of blue light rose to the ceiling and then crashed on her body, turning the ice crystals blue and making them colder. Penny pressed the coins on her eyelids and exhaled.

"I don't know what's wrong with them tonight, but their snoring buzzsaws."

Penny waved a finger, and a soft breeze pushed against her feet, turning her body until her head pointed at the window, away from the noise. She tried again to sleep, but when she felt her body drifting away, the snoring returned, interrupting her again.

"At this point, I may as well be sleeping in a volcano," she snapped.

After repositioning herself a second time, Penny concentrated on her breathing. Finally, the sounds of the world started drifting away. When the sounds of her sisters' snoring became white noise, Penny peacefully exhaled and fell asleep.

For a moment, there was only darkness and complete silence. Unconsciously, Penny reached up and touched the coins on her eyelids. Suddenly, a lightning bolt came out of the ceiling and struck Penny in the chest, knocking the coins covering her eyes to the floor. The jolt of electricity opened Penny's eyelids to reveal her eyeballs were gone; in their place, two small whirlpools of radiant energy. Penny closed her eyes for a brief moment before opening them again. When she did, Penny was flying through the sky like a rocket.

Penny was different now. Her vibrant, youthful body was gone, replaced by one reflecting her actual age; she was hundreds of years old. Her long, luxurious locks were nowhere to be found. She was bald now except for a few strands of white hair around her ears. The only places Penny had an abundance of hair were the two places most women didn't want growth - her eyebrows and chin; the eyebrows were so gray and bushy that they hung down over her eyelids, partially blocking her vision, while the stubble on her chin stuck out like a porcupine. The skin on Penny's face was old and wrinkled like a used baseball glove, and there were huge bags under her eyes. All her teeth had fallen out, and there was so much bone loss that her face looked like it was caving in on itself.

The witch was a blur of wind as she flew through the clouds, and there was no indication that the deterioration of her body affected her. She flew over mountains so fast that the sky rumbled with thunder. Penny continued pushing higher in the sky until she saw the stars shimmering in space like jewels on a necklace. Soon, it was hard for Penny to breathe, but she didn't care. She continued pushing, wanting to see how close she could get. Her sister warned her on numerous occasions about flying too close to space. She remembered the conversation she had with Indigo.

"I know what you do when you sleep at night," said Indigo one day while washing her clothes in the stream.

"What?" asked Penny, feigning innocence.

"Look, I know."

Penny turned away from her sister and scrubbed her clothes against a stone.

"I don't know what you're talking about."

"I'm your sister, Penny. Did you think you could hide your room of Kish at the bottom of the Atlantic, and we wouldn't know? We all have rooms. Mine is in the Mayon volcano in the Philippines. Inez has one atop Mount Everest."

Penny snickered.

"I know. Inez woke up one morning with snow in her panties. We're supposed to use the rooms for building spells. What was Inez doing up there?"

"Cut the shit, Penny. We're talking about you. I know what you do when you travel to your Kish. I saw it in a vision."

"It's harmless."

"Stop doing it."

"Why?"

"They might see you."

"You don't see anything wrong with Heaven watching us like we're a tv show?"

"They don't watch us, and they don't know where we are. And we should keep it that way."

"Yeah, but..."

"When you draw near to leaving earth's atmosphere, who knows what kinds of alarms that raises in Heaven? We can't see inside their domain, so we have no idea who may be watching. And if they discover what we're doing, they'll punish us."

Suddenly, Penny returned to reality. The sting of her tongue splitting from the cold air made her concentrate. She quickly closed her mouth and stared out into space. The idea of being discovered by one of Heaven's angels excited Penny. Although she knew what would happen if she or her sisters got caught, Penny couldn't resist flying to the edge of the earth's atmosphere to glare at those who might be watching. It was her way of saying "fuck you" to the system, to those with the power to take her life, a life she'd abandoned her mother's Christianity and learned witchcraft to preserve.

As Ice crystals formed on her old face, Penny smiled, her toothless face twisting like an amoeba as if the bones inside were gone. Her thin lips cracked, and the skin peeled away as she drew closer to space. Just when Penny was about to leave Earth, the witch turned her body and flew back toward the Earth so fast that the skin on her face burst into flame. As Penny descended, the air around her body ignited, making her body burn like a meteor shooting out of the sky. As the air around her grew hotter and hotter, Penny spotted her marker - a large, waterless black cloud hovering in the storm's center.

"There she goes," whispered Penny. "Time to get to work."

Penny flew into the cloud so fast that a huge column of water reached up from the sea and hit her in the chest. The impact of the water sent the witch twirling like a top. Penny used the momentum to spin faster and faster until a great whirlpool formed in the center of the ocean. The water continued churning until a massive hole appeared in the ocean's center that stretched for miles. Penny extended her arms like a bird and stopped above the crater. Finally, she tucked her hands to her sides and started falling. As Penny fell down the shaft, the old woman looked to her right and saw an enormous sperm whale staring back at her. She looked to her left and saw sharks, dolphins, and a gigantic octopus zoom by, all circling the edges of the whirlpool, unable to free themselves.

"Calm down. I'll be out of your hair shortly," Penny whispered.

As Penny continued falling, the spray from the sides of the whirlpool extinguished her burning body. With the fire out, it took a while for the witch's eyes to adjust to the light. Still, when they did, she saw the same terrifying creatures caught up in her whirlpool that she'd seen on previous trips: an enormous white snake with a head the size of a small bus filled with dozens of long sharp teeth that glowed when it bit down on its prey; a hammerhead shark that Penny nicknamed "Betsy the Bitch". There was a hole in the top of its body where the dorsal fin was supposed to be. Half the shark's face was missing, and it seemed helpless in the current, allowing it to carry it here and there while its only eye darted from side to side, searching for predators that could take advantage of its injury.

And then, there was the enormous jellyfish that Penny nicknamed "Chuck." The jellyfish usually lay on the ocean floor, waiting in the darkness. The creature lay motionless for days, pretending to be a part of the ocean floor, until something big swam close, and it shot up a clear liquid that instantly paralyzed it. Before the stunned creature realized what was happening, the jellyfish had smothered it to death and ingested it in its thick, slimy body. Penny didn't like to disturb the creatures with her periodic visits, but she had no choice. The water funnel was her only way to gain entrance, so the animals had to deal with it until she reached her destination.

Soon, darkness swallowed everything, and Penny heard the thundering currents pushing against the walls of water. When the creatures in the ocean began attacking the funnel walls, Penny snapped her fingers and spoke inside her mind.

"Mik-tu-ooosh"

Penny's body transformed into water, and the walls of the whirlpool came crashing in. The force of the ocean would've been enough to destroy anything, but it didn't harm the witch. The water passed through Penny's body like a gentle breeze, and she calmly stepped onto the ocean floor. Penny snapped her finger again, and her cheeks started to glow. She slowly opened her mouth, and a small bubble made of light came out. As the orb rose to the surface, it allowed Penny to gather her bearings. A few meters above, she saw the angry whale and shark swimming in her direction.

"Aw, calm down," said Penny. "It didn't take as long as the last time. You'll be okay."

The whale lumbered overhead, seemingly accepting the witch's explanation before taking off in another direction. Penny looked to her right and saw Betsy The Bitch speeding in her direction. The disfigured hammerhead shark was a little more annoyed by Penny's prison of water, and it swam at Penny to register her complaint. Penny closed her eyes as the shark passed through her body. When she opened her eyes, she saw the shark swimming away.

"You need to get a life, Betsy. You're too serious, girl," Penny snapped.

Satisfied that the creature wouldn't return, Penny murmured again, and her body returned to human form. She looked around until she spotted her makeshift house. Penny raised her hand and mumbled another spell – this time, a giant bubble filled with white light came out of her mouth and followed overhead as she moved through the water. With the sphere bathing the ocean floor in white light, Penny swam across the ocean floor until she reached the Kish.

Penny built the Kish with different pieces of rock. But these weren't just any stone; they had unique mystical energy. Penny collected some of the rocks inside burning volcanoes. A few seconds before the volcanos erupted, Penny dashed in and cast the Pluto Spell, which turned her hands into ice blocks. When the volcano erupted, Penny dunked her hands into the molten lava. When the ice from Pluto mixed with the magma, a reaction caused the volcano to shoot sheets of shiny black rock high into the air. Penny hid from the falling debris until she spotted a sheet of rock she liked.

But the other way Penny gathered stones for her Kish was one she hated – foraging dreams. Searching the dreams of unsuspecting people was dangerous for many reasons; there were beasts so vicious and unpredictable that Penny barely survived. No two creatures were the same, and all possessed power rivaling her own. When she saw one of the stones she needed, Penny couldn't just grab it. She had to wait for a diversion or surprise to divert the monster's attention. Penny often had to hide for hours underneath the snow, in wells and toilets filled with excrement, waiting for the right time to grab her dream stone. Sometimes she saw the stone, and sometimes she didn't. There were times when the rock would glow and emit a sound that told her where it was hiding, but other times, Penny instinctively ran to where she guessed the stone was. The whole experience was a terrifying ordeal that yielded too few results. It was easy to get lost in someone's dream and not be able to find your way home for days or weeks. But eventually, after fifty years of running through nightmares, Penny found enough rock for her Kish.

When connected and shaped into a functional Kish, all the stones provided what Penny needed: protection from the attacks of thieving witches, mystics too lazy to learn sorcery through trial and error, and who only wanted to steal from others with more talent. Penny didn't understand why or how she knew, but the magic from the dreams and volcanoes kept her Kish hidden from all the witches except her sisters. Penny didn't care that her sisters knew; she only cared that her spells were safe from those who would bring harm.

Penny's Kish was a special place to her. Although she knew the primary function of the Kish, Penny used it as a multipurpose room; sometimes, Penny used it to escape her annoying sisters, and other times, she used it to sit in darkness and think about her mom. But mostly, Penny used the Kish exactly as the Oracle instructed – as a place to experiment and grow her book of witchery.

There were no windows or doors. The Kish appeared partially buried on the ocean floor, but it wasn't; after each of her visits, Penny intentionally used her magic to cover the edges of the building with sand, a marker that told her if someone had been there. To protect the sea life from the poisons that sometimes flooded the Kish because of her experiments, Penny created a different conjuration that produced unlimited algae. Hungry barnacles traveled from all around the ocean to feast on the algae. Eventually, the barnacles died, leaving their hardened shells, forming an even more powerful protective barrier that prevented Penny's witchery from poisoning the ocean.

Penny continued floating before the Kish, ensuring all was safe. To be sure no one was there, she swam around the building, looking for disturbances in the sand. Finally, satisfied that all was okay, Penny swam out to a large clump of bushes a few feet from the structure; hidden beneath the brush was a passage she had dug to access the hut. Penny waved her hand over the bush, which rolled away to reveal a tunnel. Penny swam above the hole and prepared to speak the spell that would suck her inside.

But suddenly, she stopped.

The sand she'd been standing on seemed to move like something was pushing at it to get out. Penny was startled until she remembered the giant jellyfish she'd trapped in the whirlpool.

"Damn it, Chuck," said Penny in her head. "I know you're mad, but the whirlpool didn't hurt you that much, did it?"

Penny continued staring at the sand as it made waves that mimicked the ocean. She waited for Chuck's customary acknowledgment of a truce – whipping up the sand in a cloud before shooting ink at her before swimming away.

But nothing happened.

Penny was about to swim down and stir the sand on the ocean floor to get Chuck's attention when she suddenly became disoriented; the ocean seemed to be moving in one giant wave, and she could not buoy herself. Soon, a new fear appeared - Penny felt her powers slipping away. Suddenly, she was struggling to hold herself underwater. Penny looked up and saw the bubble of light drifting back to the surface. As the light faded, Penny started to panic – she was lost and didn't know where she was.

"What kind of devilment is this?" she asked.

Penny tried to remain calm, but she couldn't. Something evil was in the water, and it wanted her dead. She could feel it. The witch closed her eyes and tried using her powers to sense movement in the water.

"Come on, where are you?" she asked.

But Penny couldn't concentrate. For some reason, her powers were dull and unbalanced, like stumbling through a dark room. Time was running out. She'd surely succumb to mortal death if she didn't eliminate the enemy hiding in the ocean. Her lungs were on fire, and she wanted to open her mouth for air but put the thought out of her mind. She could feel the pressure of the sea squeezing her body like a vice, her head pounding inside like someone was hitting her head with a sledgehammer.

"I've got to.... concentrate," she thought.

Still, the pressure within the ocean squeezed her body relentlessly, eventually making her legs throb in agony.

"Fuck!" she yelled as she felt the bones in her legs break in half.

Penny reached down to grab her legs and a new arthritic pain shot through her spine, and she twisted in agony.

"Ahhhh! Mother of Orashu, please help me!" pleaded Penny, taking in a mouthful of salty water.

But she was alone in the ocean's cold depths, and no one but evil was there for her. Penny was a frantic mess. She tried remembering a spell to stop the pain from drowning her soul, but her thoughts were a grain of sand lost on a beach. A new idea entered her head, and she began searching for the creatures she'd trapped in the whirlpool.

"Chuck! Betsy!" she cried out with her mind. "Anyone! Help!"

Realizing she could die, Penny started crying. The weight of the sea was upon her head again, squeezing it, making her brain burn. Penny opened her mouth to alleviate the rising force in her ears when suddenly one of her eyeballs popped out of her skull. Half Penny's world immediately turned black while blood rose before her face. Penny quickly grabbed the orb of flesh and tried to push her eyeball back inside her skull, but it wouldn't fit. She looked around for nearby sharks and felt relief when she saw none. But Penny knew the ways of the ocean; the smell of her blood would draw ocean predators to her location immediately.

With only half her sight and blood leaking from her skull, Penny put her eyeball inside her mouth and swam around in a circle, searching for the entrance to her Kish. Finally, she spotted the bush, and relief rushed through her. A feeling of dread overcame her as she swam through the water to the hole. Penny turned around suddenly and looked back into the dark ocean.

"No."

Suddenly, the seafloor exploded. The force of the blast was so powerful it lifted huge chunks of stone out of the sand and hurled them toward the surface. Penny dodged the rocks as they shot up from the bottom. She quickly tried to swim into her tunnel, but the passageway had caved in, and there was no way to escape. There was another explosion, and all the sand on the seafloor shot up. This time, Penny could not evade the projectiles as they rose from beneath her; the water immediately became a black cloud of sand and stones, smashing into Penny's legs and stripping her of the ability to see. A gigantic rock rose from the seafloor and crashed into Penny's legs with such force that it knocked the wind out of her lungs and almost made her spit out the eyeball she was carrying in her mouth.

Unable to escape the madness around her, Penny accepted her fate. She closed her eyes and prepared to let the seawater flood her lungs. Suddenly, a bright light shot up from the ocean floor. Penny looked down and almost screamed – the explosion revealed a pit filled with lava and burning hot coals that stretched as far as she could see, all filled with thousands of red-skinned three-headed demons. As the monsters climbed over one another, they snatched nearby sea animals from the water and ate them. The heat from the chasm of hell made the whole ocean boil like a hot cauldron, instantly cooking the nearby sea life. Soon, the heat reached Penny. But something happened to the witch; she could think again and felt her powers return. Penny became angry at what she was witnessing; although she had her disagreements with the creatures of the ocean, she considered them her friends. Now, they were all dead, cooked by something from hell.

"Bus-ki-ti-ti," Penny chanted inside her mind.

Penny waved her hand, and large sheets of ice surrounded her body. Although she was still in the water, Penny felt comfortable that she had enough protection from the heat to perform the spell. She opened her mouth and spat her eyeball into the ocean. Instead of the eyeball floating away, it hovered in front of Penny. Penny started convulsing, and her face became as dark as soot. Her bald head instantly grew blonde hair until it was as long as a sea snake. The locks wrapped around Penny's body and squeezed her tightly.

"Bus-ki-ti-ti," the witch repeated.

The blonde hair suddenly became as white as snow and sent volts of electricity into the witch's body. Penny opened her mouth and screamed.

"Ahhhhhhh!"

Although she was underwater, the scream was loud, sending shock-waves into the ocean. The white hair on Penny's body fell to the ocean floor while Penny hovered above the seabed, unconscious with her mouth open. After a while, she convulsed again, and a thick sludge shot floated from her mouth. The liquid crawled from Penny's mouth, enveloped the eyeball, and shot into the witch's empty eye socket. Penny's head filled with white light, glowing like an enormous lantern. Veins of energy appeared in her skull and moved like fire trails through her skull, down her neck, and into her body, repairing broken bones and absorbing her injuries. Finally, the light dimmed, and Penny opened her eyes.

When Penny looked down, the demons were about to grab her feet.

"Not today, assholes."

Penny extended her hands and spoke a different spell.

"Nightmares and coffee, lam-ti-copi," she chanted.

Just as Penny's body started disappearing, a demon grabbed her and tried pulling her to the bottom of the ocean.

"Too late," she said as she faded.

Penny was gone.

15

The Wrong Side of the Bed

Penny awoke with a start; she had been floating a few feet above the floor when she went to bed, but Penny woke up so suddenly that she forgot and crashed to the floor.

"Fuck!" she yelled, with pain radiating through her back.

As the pain subsided, Penny sat up and opened her eyes. Although all the lights were out, the room was as hot as fire. But there were no flames. Penny put her hands on the floor and immediately winced in pain; the wooden floor was as hot as coals. Suddenly, Penny felt a new pain – something was squeezing her legs like a vice. Penny tried to grab her legs, but the squeezing grew tighter as soon as she moved.

"What the hell is going on?" she whispered.

Penny remembered her last moments in the dream world and became nervous – she remembered the demon at the bottom of the ocean reaching out for her just as she left. Penny opened her eyes as wide as she could and tried to look around the room without moving. But the room was as dark as ink, and Penny couldn't see anything. Deciding to rely on her senses, Penny stopped moving and held her breath to see if the monster had somehow crossed the dreamscape portal and was in the room with her. Penny sat motionless, waiting for something to move in the darkness. After ten minutes of sitting silently, she released her breath. Nothing was there. Penny quickly ran her hands over her body. Aside from the throbbing in her legs, her body was young again, and there were no other injuries or traces of old age. The spell of youth was intact.

Penny ran her fingers down her legs and felt the wetness of blood just below her kneecap. Afraid of how bad her injuries were, she yelled for her sisters.

"Inez! Indigo!"

Suddenly, a rustling noise sounded at her feet, and Penny jumped. There came another swishing sound from the right and the left. Penny lifted her palms in front of her face and spoke the words of battle.

"Eqim-ver-ton-plais-ko-lo."

A blue flame rose from Penny's palms and engulfed her body. As the light from the fire grew, she could see what was in the room.

"Holy shit!"

Penny was sitting in the center of a room filled with the same evil plants she'd seen in the forest. The plant life from hell covered everything, and Penny barely recognized what had once been her bedroom. There were towering plants and small ones. Some plants were beautiful with inviting colors, while others had menacing appearances that told of their murderous intent. Penny deduced that some of the plants on the walls were born of spores that rode in the nighttime breeze. Others had all but attacked Penny's bedroom, tearing big holes in the walls and ripping open the ceiling like canned tuna.

Some of the plants mimicked regular foliage, while others were so strange that Penny couldn't believe her eyes; on the far side of the room, a yellow bulb in the center of a strangely shaped flower dripped a red liquid that burned a massive hole in the floor. Penny watched in astonishment as the liquid dripped from the flower in sync with her breathing; when she stopped, the liquid stopped. All the plants seemed to connect to her life force somehow; if Penny blinked, the flower on her right bent and shivered before returning upright. Another flower, a chubby purple tulip-like plant with dozens of spikes on its petals, seemed to dare Penny to move and leaned in her direction whenever she turned her head.

But the most terrifying thing Penny saw was standing before her – a glass tree with dozens of twisted and distorted branches that were all reaching out for her!

Penny lost her breath at the sight of the foliage. In all her years of living as a witch, she'd never witnessed something so sinister, so disturbing to her soul. Penny tried to dampen her fear by turning away from the tree, but she couldn't remove her eyes; although there was no sound, Penny could feel the tree beckoning her, inviting her to submit to its will.

"What *are* you?" whispered Penny.

The tree shivered, and crystal chimes rang throughout the room. The sound caused a fresh pain in Penny's legs, and she winced in agony. That's when she noticed it; at the center of the plant was a giant black hole – and Penny's feet were inside!

"No," whimpered Penny.

Once again, the crystal chimes responded to the sound of Penny's voice by ringing. The pain in Penny's legs returned and radiated like fire. She closed her eyes in agony and waited until the pain subsided. After the noise disappeared, Penny opened her eyes and stared at the hole in the tree. After a few moments of looking at the mystical tree, Penny jumped in surprise and almost screamed at what she saw; the hole in the tree wasn't a hole at all – it was a mouth! The tree was eating her, inching forward and taking her legs into its mouth. Inside the dark hole were its teeth - glass daggers that stabbed Penny's calves and pulled her in, sucking the blood leaking from her legs.

Penny could barely control herself. What she had felt in her dream at the bottom of the ocean wasn't an attack from the demons but from the real world. The drain of her powers was an alert for her to wake up and return to defend herself before the tree consumed her body.

"Ginni-ein-libc-weee-fep," chanted Penny. "Hern-horo-Nim-Kim!"

Suddenly, a powerful force jerked Penny from the mouth of the tree, tearing off pieces of her leg before lifting her high.

"Ahhhhh!" she screamed as blood sprayed from her wounds.

Penny heard something flying through the air and remembered the menacing thorn-covered plant that mimicked her movements. She immediately pushed outward with her spirit, causing the blue fire surrounding her body to become a blazing inferno. The needles on the plant on the other side of the room crashed into the fire and melted away. While dangling in the air, Penny whispered another spell.

"Heal me, Utisma, for all is whole in the center of the universe. Oma-shi-ja!"

The wounds on Penny's legs closed, and the crushed bones became whole again. Grateful that the pain was gone, Penny closed her eyes and sighed in relief.

But she forgot the other plants in the room. The destruction of the plant's poisonous arrows made the other plants aggressive. The leaves on the plants started to shake wildly, sending toxic spores into the air. Other plants opened to reveal creatures hidden inside. The large plant that shot poisonous darts at Penny opened its leaves and released a toxic gas. Several nearby plants reacted to the steam and opened to reveal an army of strange insects hidden inside. The insects screamed and took off, flying towards Penny. After a few seconds, the plant that released the gas exploded, and a growling monster with purple skin climbed out of its thick stem. The creature hissed like a snake when it saw Penny floating in the air. It raised its tiny paw and chewed off its arm before running full speed to attack the witch. Penny saw the creature and shouted.

"Enough!"

Penny shot up through the structure's roof and circled the house. When she had enough speed, Penny flew around in a tight, counterclockwise motion, spinning slowly at first, then aiming the tips of her toes at the hole above her bedroom. As the cold, disgusting rain splashed against her face, Penny focused on the hell in her bedroom.

"You fuckers are out of here!" she screamed, flying faster and faster.

Penny spun in reverse in the center of a tornado and started sucking all the plant life out of the building.

"If you want war, you got it!" screamed Penny.

The force of the wind lifted a winged demonic creature covered in mud from the room. The monster was bigger than the others and fought against the wind ferociously, its purple wings flapping as it tried to escape. When Penny saw the beast hovering, she clapped her hands and spoke a spell.

"From the darkness comes fire!" she screamed.

Suddenly, the tornado was a blazing funnel of wind and fire, burning everything inside. Penny kept her hands interlocked as she continued spinning inside the fire tornado. Soon, a long line of fire extended like a rope from her clasped hands and became a giant hand made of fire. The burning hand reached out and grabbed the monster by the throat.

"You have no idea of the power I possess," screamed Penny, with flames dancing in her eyes

Although she was a witch, Penny was a wild banshee of flame and anger, her hair ablaze in an orange and yellow fire. She was tired of being pushed around by all the forces of good and evil. It was time for her to let everyone know who she was and the power she wielded.

Penny continued spinning while holding the beast in the funnel's center as the monster struggled to free itself, throttling it with her magical hands. Finally, Penny grabbed the monster's head and squeezed – the monster shrieked, and a disgusting crunch sounded as the witch crushed its skull. Penny let go of the body, and the wind sucked the body up with the other plants.

Penny used the tornado of fire to suck each of the demons and plant life from hell out of her house. As the creatures flew past her in a whirl of confusion, their skin sizzling in flames, Penny saw their hideous faces and flashed a sinister smile. She wanted each demonic monster to see her face and know who she was.

"Tell your fucking master who sent you back to hell! Remember my face!" she yelled as they flew by.

One by one, Penny saw each monster- the hairy snakes, the miniature devils, insects with flaming wings, three-headed bats, skinless snakes with glowing intestines for bodies – and extracted them all from her room. Finally, after she had captured the last creature in her funnel of fire, Penny rose into the sky and pointed her finger towards a nearby lake.

"Go back to hell!" she screamed.

The tornado disconnected from Penny's body and spun away towards the lake. The fire ceased burning, and the funnel lowered its tail into the center of the water.

"Payback is a bitch, ain't it?" asked Penny as she gleefully watched the tornado pin the monsters underwater.

There was a great splashing of water as the monsters tried to free themselves, but Penny's power was too great; she held the group of monsters underwater until the splashing ceased, and she was sure all her enemies were dead. Finally, Penny waved her hand, and the tornado disappeared. But she stayed floating in the air, watching the lake. Soon, a corpse floated to the surface, then another and another, until the top of the lake looked like a cemetery of freaks.

Penny remembered her sisters and flew down from the sky into her room.

"Inez! Indigo!" yelled Penny.

Penny froze - Inez was inside a glass tree filled with green liquid, holding her breath and banging against the glass covering.

"Hold on, Inez. I'll get you out!" yelled Penny.

As she moved past a toppled table toward Inez, Penny noticed long strands of hair sticking out from a corner. Slowly, she inched closer. Finally, Penny saw what was lying on the floor - her sister Indigo was lying flat on her back, staring at the ceiling.

"Indi!" she mouthed in silence.

Suddenly, Indigo's chest moved, and her head fell to the side. The witch stared at Penny with glassy eyes while pink foam poured out of her mouth. Penny was about to help her but paused suddenly; Indigo's body moved again, this time more forceful as though something was pulling her. Slowly, Penny peered around the corner to see what was happening.

A muscular creature with red skin and an enormous head stood over Indigo. The monster had two massive wings on its back and dozens of horns sticking out of its body. Although the creature seemed to be standing on two legs, Penny realized the monster had four legs; each leg was thin and muscular, attached by thick reptilian skin. The beast had huge, hairy hands with sharp claws resembling knives. Its eyes constantly moved in circles, scanning the ceiling, floor, and ceiling again as though it were searching for its next meal.

Penny moved back. She tried to think of a spell to save her sister, but she couldn't concentrate because she was scared; she'd never seen her sister so close to death and didn't know what to do. Penny peeked out again and almost screamed. The monster had one of Indigo's half-eaten legs in its mouth and was tearing the remaining flesh from the thigh with its teeth while releasing a high-pitched scream that sounded like a bird.

Penny looked at her sister and saw the paleness of death draining the blood out of her face. Indigo looked at her and gave a faint smile before closing her eyes. Penny knew she only had a few minutes before her sister would die.

Suddenly, Penny remembered a spell she'd worked on in her Kish in the ocean. She stepped out of hiding and ran full speed at the monster.

"From the mud! Hod-kur-air!" she yelled.

There was a flash of light, and Penny's body replicated into three different witches. All three replicas froze and turned to brown clay before bursting into flame. The monster dropped the leg and immediately attacked, slashing with its claws and growling as the other two figures reached out and grabbed its arms. The beast never noticed the fourth object, a shadow on the wall that was Penny in disguise. As the monster attacked, the clay figures started clinging to one another. They were unrecognizable and became a giant blob of brown mud and sticky glue within seconds. The monster bit at the mess, trying to free itself, but the bond became tighter the more it struggled. Penny stepped off the wall and reappeared in her original body. As the monster growled, trying to free itself, the witch walked to her sister and kneeled by her side. Penny placed her hand over Indigo's chest and shot a blast of energy into her heart.

"You're not dying today, Indi," she whispered.

Penny cupped both her hands over her mouth and blew into her fist. A small white cloud hovered in the air when she lowered her hand, and Penny grabbed it and put it over Indigo's nose and mouth.

"Use this to breathe. I'll be back."

Penny ran past the struggling pile of mud on the floor and past a few plants to the strange tree where Inez was slowly drowning inside. Penny guessed the liquid was acid because half of Inez's face was hanging down like it was melting and her hair was gone, replaced by huge purple blisters were on her skull.

"I've got you, Inez! Get away from the glass!"

Penny raised her fist and shot a blast of energy at the tree. Suddenly, there was a loud hiss in the room, and thousands of bugs poured into the liquid, attacking Inez.

"Inez!" screamed Penny.

Penny flew up and tore the roof off the house. She aimed at the crystal tree with her glowing fists and clasped her hands together. Once again, the hand of fire appeared. Penny reached down and lifted the tree into the sky. She tried tearing the tree open with her hand of fire, but the material of the tree was too strong for her magic. Penny looked inside and saw her sister firing relentlessly at the insects, trying to melt them with her magic. Her entire face was drooping now, and her skin color was grey.

Suddenly, Penny got an idea. She lowered the tree to the apartment and landed in front of it. Penny extinguished her hand and moved closer, pulling up her sleeve to reveal her skin. As soon as she got close enough, the bottom of the tree opened, and two pale hands reached out, trying to grab her and pull her inside.

"Just as I suspected," whispered Penny. "Come here, you fucker!"

Penny blinked, and her hands became two metal clasps. She reached down and locked her arms around the two arms sticking out of the tree.

"Gotcha!"

Penny pulled on the arms, but the creature was strong. Its body remained hidden underneath the tree as she struggled to get it out. Penny looked at her sister inside the tree, firing bursts of fire at the insects surrounding her.

"*Inez!*" Penny said inside her mind. "*Fire at the base of the tree!*"

Inez nodded her head in agreement. As she floated in the toxic fluid, Inez aimed at the tree's base and fired a continuous burst of fire. Penny felt the monster's grip loosen.

"*It's working! Keep shooting!*"

Suddenly, Penny yanked with all her might and fell back, pulling the monster out of its hiding place. She saw the demon and quickly rose to her feet.

"Holy shit!"

The demon looked like a man from its head to its waist, but there were no legs. Instead, the bottom portion of its body was made of thousands of glowing beetles, all hissing and moving.

"Feed," the creature moaned.

Penny watched as the thousands of beetles attached to the demon formed two legs and lifted it off the ground. The monster opened its mouth, and hundreds of bugs swarmed out its throat toward Penny.

"Hungry?" asked Penny, her arms transforming back into hands made of fire. "Eat on this!"

The witch raised her hand and shot two fire blasts into the creature's mouth. The monster stumbled back in surprise, and its head fell back.

It struggled to raise its head for a few moments before the head fell entirely off, landing on the floor and turning into a pile of bugs—the insects no longer with a master scattered throughout the room.

Penny ran to the tree and reshot the glass trunk – this time, the tree exploded, and her sister came tumbling out. With her face sagging, Inez vomited before slowly rising to her feet. She raised her head, placed both palms on her face, and cast a spell.

"Inside and out. Return the soul. Trop-mir-leeee,"

Light flashed inside Inez's palm, igniting her skin before the magical green fire crawled through her skull, down her neck, and into her body. After a few seconds, she lifted her head, her face healed.

"Indigo! Where is she?"

The two witches ran to their sister. When they arrived, Indigo was just as Penny left her, a bubble of magic covering her face with her half-eaten legs sprawled on the floor. The monster that attacked Indigo was gone - suffocated and consumed by the ball of sticky black magic. The only thing remaining was a black spot on the floor.

"Indigo! Are you okay?" asked Inez.

Indigo tossed aside the small cloud over her face and coughed – blood shot out of her mouth.

"I'll be okay," she replied.

Inez kneeled in front of her sister.

"Don't worry about the legs, Sis. You can live without them."

Penny's mouth fell open.

"What the fuck did you say?"

Inez shot Penny a worried look and motioned for her sister to be quiet.

"This whole thing is sickening!" continued Penny.

"Penny, stop! Indigo is...."

"Fuck you, Inez. This war has gone on long enough! I'm going to cancel the spell."

Indigo shook her head.

"No, Penny! There's a process. You can't just cancel the spell."

"Why not? We started it to prevent the demons from taking over and to gain power. But it backfired! None of this is worth dying for!"

Indigo shot a worried look at Inez.

"We have to tell her," said Indigo.

Penny looked from Indigo to Inez, confused.

"Tell me what?"

Inez shook her head.

"We can't speak about it. The Oracle told us that if we...."

"What choice do we have? You have to tell her before she does something stupid."

Inez walked over and grabbed Penny's arm.

"There's a reason no one has ever used the spell."

"Yeah, I know. You already explained."

"No, there's something else – a prophecy."

Penny looked at both her sisters in disbelief.

"You two and your fucking secrets. What is it this time?"

Inez took a deep breath.

"The Oracle told us whoever stops the spell prematurely will be marked for death."

"Prematurely?"

"The spell went untouched for thousands of years because of what it does. It attaches to your soul and becomes a part of you permanently."

"I don't understand."

"It's a living, breathing entity that entered our lives as soon as we cast the spell. It made terrible things happen to us because it wants us to interfere with its intended purpose. Indigo lost her legs, and I almost drowned; it was all intentional. The storm wants us to stop it."

"Why?"

"The Oracle doesn't know."

"And what happens if we stop it."

"Heaven."

"Heaven? What about it?"

"The storm attaches a permanent marker to your soul that tells Heaven precisely who initiated the spell."

"I'm not worried about that. Heaven will have to catch me first."

Inez slapped her sister's face.

"Stop fucking around and grow up! Don't you get it? Heaven will hold us responsible for everything that's happened. If that storm places that marker, Heaven will send us all to Hell!"

But Penny wasn't listening. She angrily shoved Inez and sent her sailing across the room. Inez almost crashed into the wall, but she raised her hand, and her magic stopped her momentum.

"I've told you, Inez, keep your goddamned hands to yourself!" yelled Penny.

"Forget you! Maybe it's time I teach you a lesson!" replied Inez.

Inez flew across the room to attack Penny when a large bookcase rose from across the room and crashed between them. Surprised, they turned to Indigo.

"Why don't both of you cut the shit!"

"She hit me first!"

"Forget you! You're so immature sometimes!"

Indigo raised her palm.

"R-rejuvenation," she stuttered, her hands bursting into flames.

Indigo glared at her sisters while pressing her burning hands on her wounds, searing them and sending smoke into the air. The smell of burning flesh disgusted Inez, and she almost vomited while Penny watched with tears streaming down her face.

"Indi, I'm sorry. I..."

Indigo winced in agony as she pressed the magic flames against her open wounds.

"We don't have time for this. Look, Penny, you can't stop the rain because...."

Suddenly, Indigo closed her eyes.

"Indigo!" yelled Inez. "What is it?"

Suddenly, a deep growl rang out in the room.

"What is it?" asked Penny.

"I don't know!" replied Inez.

Indigo started spinning around uncontrollably. Her body smashed against the wall repeatedly before landing on the floor. Inez tried to grab her, but something lifted her off the ground and spun her again.

"Indigo!" yelled Penny.

Penny tried to grab her sister's arm, but Indigo was spinning too fast. Unconscious, she smashed into the ceiling before crashing to the floor for the second time. Before she moved again, Penny jumped on top of her and held her down.

"I got you, Indi."

Penny held Indigo down while Inez placed her hand on the crown of Indigo's head and released a burst of energy.

"It's okay, Indigo. Sleep. You're safe."

Suddenly, a thick black vein appeared at the corner of Indigo's eye, and It moved across the bridge of her nose, breaking it and shooting down her neck.

"What the hell?" asked Inez.

Both sisters watched in horror as something moved inside Indigo's body.

"That's it!" yelled Penny. "This ends now!"

Inez tried grabbing Penny's arm, but she missed.

"Penny, no! You don't understand!"

Penny shot through the roof and into the rainy night sky.

16

Gathering Souls

8:00 am

Smith Residence

Greg stood in his basement, peering out of the small window. Although it was morning, everything was black, darkened by the endless rain soaking the city for a week. He opened his rifle and checked to ensure he had ammunition before running his finger along his waist; the two pistols were in his belt.

"Daddy?"

Greg turned around and saw a small figure sitting upright on a cot in the rear of the room.

"Tabitha, go back to sleep."

"I can't, Daddy. When is Mommy coming back?"

Greg sighed and walked to his daughter. After propping his rifle against the water heater, he sat down on the bed and hugged her.

"You have to sleep, baby."

"I can't. Where's Mommy?"

Greg grabbed the moldy pillow from the bed and placed it on his lap.

"Here, lie down on my lap."

"I can't sleep on that thing. It smells like Grandpa."

"I know, but you have to use the pillow so you don't get headaches."

"Why can't I go upstairs to my room?"

"We have to stay here for a while, okay?"

"But what about Chuck-Chuck? He needs food."

Feeling frustrated, Greg sighed.

"Don't worry about Chuck-Chuck, okay? I gave him a big bowl of food."

This statement seemed to relax the child, and she placed her head on the pillow. Greg grabbed his old, ragged Army blanket from the cot and covered Tabitha's tiny body.

"Where is Mommy, Daddy?" the child asked again.

Greg stroked his daughter's hair and stared at the tiny window on the other side of the room. He didn't have the heart to tell the child what happened. They had been in the kitchen making dinner when they heard a child's laughter in the backyard. His wife, Emma, assumed their daughter had disobeyed her instructions to sleep and had snuck outside to feed the dog.

"You see? That's your daughter, mimicking what she sees her father doing," said Emma.

"Aw, lighten up," said Greg, stealing a meatball from the pan. "Tabitha's only had that puppy for two weeks and wants to play with it."

As soon as she stepped onto the back porch, an eerie giggling rang out from the forest. Greg knew it wasn't his daughter and tried to warn his wife.

"Emma! That's not..."

Before Greg finished his sentence, he saw an enormous monster run out of the forest and grab his wife. Greg had never seen something so disgustingly terrifying. The towering monster had huge eyes the size of plates and four muscular arms. It ran to Emma and wrapped two of its arms around her waist. Before Greg could respond, the monster ripped off Emma's head and tossed her body aside. With her spinal cord still attached to her head, the beast opened its arms, and its chest peeled open. Two additional human heads burst out, flailing like tentacles on an octopus. With one of its blood-covered hands, the monster grabbed Emma's spinal cord and shoved it inside the opening in its body. There was a metallic click, and soon Emma's head was alive, slithering with the others, menacing scowls on their faces.

Gregg ducked behind the kitchen wall as the monster searched for more victims. He immediately backed away from the kitchen and crept upstairs to Tabitha's room. Gregg quietly lifted his sleeping daughter from her bed and crept downstairs to the basement. Once inside, he listened as the monster ransacked the house. The noise woke Tabitha, and the child almost screamed, but Gregg quickly put his hand over her mouth and dialed 911 on his cell phone. They sat in darkness for ten minutes, waiting for the police to come. When he heard the sirens of police vehicles approaching, Gregg was so excited he almost ran out to greet them. But suddenly, there came a rush from the forest behind their house – like a herd of buffalo breaking through the trees in a stampede. Gregg grabbed his daughter and listened in silence.

"Daddy, what's that?" Tabitha whispered.

Gregg pulled his daughter close and listened. An enormous crash sounded like a truck hitting a brick wall. Then came the screams, the sound of police officers shrieking in pain as something pulled them from their vehicles, the random firing of weapons, the empty wailing of sirens, and the ghostly flash of red lights on the grass. The police never made it to their house, and Gregg knew why - the police met the same fate as his wife.

"Daddy, when can we leave this place?" asked Tabitha.

"Soon, baby," replied Gregg.

Gregg rocked gently, trying to put his daughter to sleep, but he couldn't take his mind off what he'd witnessed. The murder of his wife felt surreal, like it happened in a dream. He remembered how Emma had opened her mouth to scream, only to have blood shoot from her mouth. Gregg remembered how her whole body shook as the monster disconnected her head from her body, that cold dead fish look on her face as her tongue hung out the side of her mouth, the gurgling noise she made as her spine left the mush that had been her body.

"Jesus," whispered Gregg, his eyes filling with tears. "Emma."

Gregg had no idea of how he and Tabitha were going to survive. The love of his life was gone, now a permanent part of the monster that destroyed their family. He was sure there were others, dozens, maybe hundreds of monsters, combing the city in search of other lives to destroy. There was nowhere they could run, no nearby family or friends. Gregg couldn't risk exploring the forest outside their home. Tabitha was only six, and there would be no way they'd escape.

Eventually, Tabitha fell asleep, and Gregg put his daughter on the cot. After waiting a few seconds to ensure his daughter wouldn't wake up, Gregg grabbed his rifle and walked to the window. Looking outside, he saw an enormous wolf pacing back and forth at the edge of his yard. Gregg didn't think much of the animal. But when the animal turned to face the house, Gregg stared at the creature in disbelief. It wasn't a wolf but an enormous dog with two heads and glowing red eyes.

"What the fuck is that?" he whispered.

The animal seemed to hear Gregg and lifted its head. Suddenly, it took off sprinting toward the house. Another pack of monster dogs emerged from the forest as it did and gave chase, all growling and barking as they ran toward the house.

Gregg moved back to his sleeping daughter with his rifle aimed at the glass.

"Tabitha!" he whispered. "Get up. We have to go!"

The first dog crashed its face through the glass, growling as it tried to push its oversized body through the tiny space. As the shards of glass sprayed everywhere, Gregg reached for his daughter.

"Tabitha! We've got to..."

Gregg froze - Tabitha was gone!

"Tabitha!" he screamed.

Gregg tossed aside the bed in search of his daughter. As soon as he did, two decaying corpses exploded from the clay.

"Uhhhhhh...."

One of the zombies grabbed Gregg's legs, and he tumbled to the ground. As he struggled to free himself, Gregg fired his rifle at the second zombie.

"Where's my daughter?" he yelled as the creature's head exploded.

Just as he eliminated one of the zombies, the dogs ripped open a large hole in the wall, and they all poured into the room. Gregg remembered and grabbed his pistols, but the dogs bit into his arms.

"Get off me!" he yelled.

Gregg punched at everything that moved. Suddenly, he felt a deep, numbing pain in his head that made his whole body numb. He reached up to touch the top of his head and felt something attached – the cold leathery skin of a dead person's face, its teeth digging into his skull. Gregg tried to get the monster off, but one of the dogs tore his arm from his shoulder. As the blood sprayed everywhere, Gregg became lightheaded. Everything was dim, like an enormous shadow had fallen over the world. Before Gregg lost consciousness, one of the four-armed monsters tore through the wall. Its large saucer eyes danced in the darkness as it stood over Gregg. It pulled the zombie off Gregg's head, but another zombie rose from the floor and clamped down with a fresh bit, this time penetrating Gregg's skull. Gregg felt icy sensations shoot through his body, and then he passed out as the zombie sucked his brains out of his skull.

17

Hell Loves Arlo

Arlo sat on the other side of the field, watching quietly as his army of zombies emerged from the darkness carrying children. One by one, the undead, covered in the blood of the children's parents, stumbled over to several large cages and dropped the crying children in front of them.

"You can't trust John," whispered a voice in Arlo's head.

Arlo turned and stared at the violet ghost figure seated beside him – it was Isadora.

"I didn't have a choice," he said with his mind. *"He has my mother."*

Arlo nodded toward the other side of the parking lot where his mother, Claire, was floating prone in the air, her body wrapped in a blanket of dark energy that changed to red whenever she moved. The skin on her scalp was blistering; one giant bubble of fluid sat just above her forehead, while the other part of her skull was red and bald from Asura's fire.

"You're only delaying the inevitable," said Isadora. *"As soon as he gets what he wants, John will kill your mother."*

Arlo nodded in agreement. He knew John's plan when he agreed to the evil partnership but could do nothing. His mother was under John's control, and Arlo had to do something to extend her life. She didn't deserve this, and Arlo knew he had to think of a plan to get her out alive.

Arlo glared at John.

"Look at him. Arrogant prick," said Arlo, angrily grinding his teeth. *"I should kill him right now."*

Isadora stared at John, and a deep growl rumbled inside her chest. Surprised, Arlo looked at the ghost and noticed half of her face melting off her skull.

"What's happening to you?" he asked nervously.

Isadora ignored his question.

"How do we kill him?" she asked angrily.

"I'm still trying to figure out a plan."

Isadora let the breeze of the storm lift her off the ground. She floated above Arlo's head briefly and then lowered herself to rest on her boyfriend's lap. The two lovers watched silently as Asura, the witch, suddenly appeared. The old woman used her powers to fly atop the metal box. As she stood watching, her hands suddenly ignited in purple fire. The light from the witch startled the children, and an audible gasp rang out, followed by cries of fear. A zombie dropped a young redheaded boy in front of the cage and backed away. Asura aimed at the child and shot him directly in the face, igniting his hair and making the young boy scream in horror. The fire spread across the child's head as the kid rolled on the ground, slapping at his face, trying to extinguish the fire. Soon, the child's entire body burst into flame and lay on the ground burning, casting a hellish purple glow across the faces of the other terrified children. A collective scream rose from the children as they watched the burning child thrashing around uncontrollably, trying to extinguish the fire. Suddenly, the fire disappeared, and the screaming subsided. When the child finally rose from the ground, he was physically and emotionally different; his eyes were black stones in his skull, and all his fear was gone, replaced by a cold, empty stupor.

"Yes, Empress," the child said in a robotic tone. "I will obey your commands."

Asura motioned for the child to enter the cage, and he did so obediently. After the child sat on the ground, Asura aimed at another child and shot the child in the face, causing the other children to scream again. This process went on continuously until the cages were full. With the final child inside, Asura jumped from the top of the cell and slammed her fists into the mud.

"My Demon Master. Paaatrobit-Ka-om!"

The ground beneath the small prison started bubbling, and the cage began shaking. Suddenly, the soil disappeared, revealing an aqua-colored river of plasma splashing beneath the ground. The cell fell into the plasma with a splash, and the river of energy swept it away.

"Where does that river of slime lead?" asked Arlo.

"It probably leads to one of the five entrances of Hell," replied Isadora.

Suddenly, the rain stopped, and Arlo looked up in the sky.

"It stopped raining," said Arlo. "I wonder what that means."

Arlo looked over at John; the boy stood and stared at the clouds.

"Asura, the rain stopped," said John.

The witch jumped down from the top of the cage and scooped up a palmful of muddy water. After running her fingertip through the brown liquid, she turned to John.

"Those bitches! They stopped the spell!"

John looked at Arlo sitting in the mud and lowered his voice.

"I knew they'd eventually betray us," said John with a chuckle. "Do you think Arlo still has his powers?"

Asura flashed a wicked smile.

"There's only one way to find out."

Asura walked to the middle of the field and turned to smile at Arlo.

"What is she doing?" Arlo asked.

Asura aimed her fists at Arlo's mother.

"I'm going to kill this worthless bitch!" Asura yelled.

Arlo rose to his feet.

"What? No! We had a deal!"

Asura cackled, and her fists started glowing.

"Stop me if you can."

The first blast of energy hit Claire's feet and ripped one of them off.

"Ahhhhh!" screamed Claire. "You fucking bitch!"

"Mom!" yelled Arlo.

Arlo shoved his hands into the mud and closed his eyes. Suddenly, the edges of the forest started shaking.

"You'll pay for that, you bitch!" Arlo growled, his eyes glowing red.

Arlo flew into the sky. With his arms extended, he hovered above Asura and spoke inside his mind.

"Kill her now!"

Suddenly, the tree line exploded, and dozens of zombies poured onto the field. The creatures saw the witch and shrieked in hunger before sprinting towards her.

"He still has control of the zombies," yelled Asura to John.

John smiled and lifted his hand.

"Okay, Arlo. That's enough."

But Arlo wasn't listening. He wanted to kill Asura for what she did to his mother. Arlo turned and saw his mother suspended in the air, blood shooting from her missing foot. She was crying uncontrollably, mouthing a phrase continuously.

"Kill me. Kill me."

The sight of his mother begging for death infuriated Arlo. With all the power inside him, he called out to all the zombies within his reach.

"Destroy John and Asura!"

The hoard of zombies tore across the field at Asura. So many monsters were running at Asura that she had to fly into the air to escape, making the hoard of zombies miss and crash to the ground in an enormous pile of rotting flesh and bones.

"Those mindless idiots are no match for the dark magic of a sorceress. Shall I demonstrate?" asked Asura.

The witch rubbed her hands together before opening her palms and blowing a kiss at the pile of monsters. The zombies turned and started biting one another like their decaying bodies were food; one monster jumped on a smaller one and bit into its face, while a child zombie grabbed the genitals of a fat man and ripped his scrotum off. One after the other, they attacked each other, biting at rancid meat and gnawing on dusty bones, causing a riot of dead against dead.

But the confusion didn't scare Arlo; it made him angrier. A sensation rose inside that was so strong black fluid shot into his throat from his decaying stomach and poured from his mouth. Arlo was beyond angry; he was rage. The witch's words stung more than the destruction she cast upon his army of zombies. He wanted, no, he needed to see her suffering just like his mother.

Arlo screamed inside.

"Evil of the past! I call you to attack!"

Suddenly, the ground beneath Asura exploded, and a gigantic zombie crawled out of the earth. The monster was different from the other undead, its skull as big as a boulder and arms so long they dragged on the ground as it ran. No skin covered its ribcage; chunks of clay were clinging to the old bones where its organs used to be.

Arlo smiled – his powers were getting stronger. He reasserted his commands to the warring zombies.

"Kill the witch!" Arlo screamed.

Like waking from a dream, the zombies looked around, startled and confused. Finally, their eyes fell on Asura, and they ran at her again. Asura hovered in the air, continuing to dodge most of the undead, when suddenly a demonic voice rang out.

"Yooooooo!"

It was the giant zombie; it had finally spotted Asura and made its way to her location. The zombie grabbed a colossal boulder and hurled it through the air. Asura easily dodged the rock and laughed at the dead creature's attempt. The zombie growled, looked around the field, and ran to two smaller zombies. It grabbed them by their ragged clothing and hurled them into the air. Asura tried to dodge the projectiles but didn't account for their movements; one of the zombies grabbed her robe and pulled the witch from the sky, making her land in the mud with a splash. The sight of the downed witch excited the zombies, and with a fresh roar, they crawled hungrily through the muddy soil toward

Asura like spiders on a corpse. The witch raised her hand just before the monsters reached her, and a protective bubble appeared. As soon as the zombies touched the energy, they shrieked in agony; their hands burst into flame, and they immediately ran to the other side of the field, clutching their damaged body parts.

A small group of zombies spotted John, watching them from the side of the cage, and rushed toward him. John sighed impatiently and turned away from the zombies.

"Asura, can you wrap this up? We have to get the children to Lord Balam."

The zombies were about to jump on John when Asura held up her hand. A transparent energy bubble enveloped John, and the zombies crashed into the energy shield. The monsters shrieked in agony as their bodies exploded in flame. Screaming, they ran away.

"Arlo!" yelled John. "Stop this!"

But Arlo couldn't stop himself. As the zombies attacked, he could feel power teeming in his body. There was something different about his abilities. He felt more powerful than before, more sinister.

"Do you feel the power inside?" asked Isadora, wrapping her ghostly arms around Arlo's waist. *"You're becoming something better."*

Isadora's hair suddenly burst into flames, and a strange red light glowed underneath her skin. She let go of her boyfriend and sailed through the air, cackling and screaming, until she hovered above John's and Asura's heads.

"Let the world see who we are! Anyone in our way will perish!" she screamed inside Arlo's head.

But John and the witch never saw or heard the wraith flying above them; Arlo was the only one who could see his deranged girlfriend and was too furious to see her madness.

Still, Isadora flew around faster, spinning out of control with her hair ablaze, cursing and pushing her boyfriend to kill John and Asura, the witch.

"Please do it! Just fucking kill them all! Please put your hands inside John's belly and pull out his guts! Both he and the old witch deserves to die! Feast on their brains!"

Suddenly, Isadora stopped flying around and looked up at the sky. A huge black cloud was overhead.

"Something's not right," said Isadora as she looked around. *"That cloud wasn't there before."*

Isadora grew nervous as she watched the cloud spread across the sky, covering everything in complete darkness.

"My love....the cloud," Isadora whispered.

But Arlo wasn't worrying about the clouds. He was watching John. He was thinking of a plan to take his revenge on the boy. As Arlo stood watching the boy once called Manuel, black stomach acid rose from inside his belly and filled his mouth with sour black fluid. Arlo used his partially chewed tongue to splash around the vomit inside his mouth before letting it drip out like syrup. John had to die. There was no other choice.

Isadora flew to Arlo's side and attempted to grab the boy, but her ghostly arm passed through his.

"We have to go, Arlo. Something's coming," she said inside his mind.

Arlo turned to look at his mother, Claire, suspended in the air, unconscious. Suddenly, Claire's leg moved, and Arlo turned his attention to her leg; a strange multicolored fluorescent plant sitting on the edge of the treeline had bent itself in Claire's direction and extended a long black vine to the woman's injured foot and wrapped itself around it. Arlo watched in disgust as the alien plant rocked slowly back and forth, appearing to be drinking the blood from Arlo's mother's wound.

"Mom," whispered Arlo.

Filled with anger, Arlo looked at the Asura and his old best friend.

"You're going to pay for this," said Arlo.

John looked at Arlo's mother floating in the air and shook his head.

"It doesn't matter. Sooner or later, everyone dies."

Arlo's eyes became silver, and an invisible force lifted him off the ground.

"And your time to die is now," yelled Arlo.

Using his power, Arlo spoke to the zombies closest to John.

"Grab him," said Arlo in his mind.

The zombies ran toward the witch and the boy. As soon as the undead touched the orbs of power surrounding John, they burst into flame.

"You were always a bit of an idiot," yelled John, laughing as the burning zombies retreated. "Didn't you see what happened to the other mindless idiots that touched this shield?"

But the diversion was all Arlo needed. Arlo grabbed the nearest zombie, ripped off its head, and slammed it in the mud.

"I am not the weakling you think I am," Arlo growled, his voice demonic.

Arlo punched holes in the zombie's chest and closed his eyes. With his fists buried in the dead man's chest, Arlo shot two bursts of energy into the creature. Although the monster was missing its head, the zombie started convulsing, and thick black liquid poured out of its neck.

"You will pay for what you have done!" screamed Arlo.

Arlo shot two more energy blasts into the zombie's body, and all the zombies around them stood and raised their heads to the sky.

"What did you do?" asked Asura, backing away.

Suddenly, all the monsters fell to the ground and started rolling in agony. Soon, an arm burst out of the chest of one of the zombies; another one of the undead screamed as its face tore in half; another's eyes burst from its skull as a fist exploded out of his throat.

"Master!" yelled Asura. "We've got to get out of here!"

But John was unable to move. He couldn't take his eyes off what he was seeing – the zombies were multiplying.

"You will pay!" screamed Arlo.

Asura ran to John and briefly lowered their forcefields to grab his arm.

"We're going to be outnumbered. Let's get out of here."

Suddenly, a loud shriek filled the air.

"AHHHHHHH!"

Asura and John spun around, trying to find the scream's source.

"What was that?" asked John.

"I don't know," replied Asura.

Once again, the scream rang out.

"AHHHHHHHH!"

Arlo turned and saw Isadora standing behind him – in her hand were two Cherry Blossom petals.

"I can't go back there," cried Isadora, her body shaking uncontrollably.

Arlo stared at the petals in Isadora's hands and instantly knew what the petals meant – the Angels were coming.

Isadora rose slightly from the ground before landing on her feet. She tried to fly away again but couldn't lift herself into the air.

"Oh, no. The Angels are coming."

Isadora's difficulties lifting herself off the ground didn't go unnoticed; Arlo saw her struggling, and now he could see other changes in his girlfriend. Isadora's appearance seemed younger, more vibrant. The girl was almost identical to when they'd been together in high school; her body no longer shifted like a translucent ghost in the breeze. Now, she seemed almost normal.

Arlo was about to mention it when a Cherry Blossom petal landed on the ground before him. Seeing the flower snapped Arlo back to reality, and he looked into the sky; the dark cloud was expanding, stretching out like fingers across the black sky. Arlo saw his mother hovering across the field.

"I gotta get Mom," he said.

Isadora's eyes widened in surprise.

"Who? Her? Leave her!"

Arlo frowned.

"What? Don't be stupid, Isadora. That's my mother. The Angels will kill her. I've got to try to save..."

"Fuck her!"

The skin on Isadora's face melted away to reveal the skull of a phantom with green eyes before the skin regenerated. Arlo realized Isadora's powers were disappearing; she could no longer manipulate her appearance. The Angels were almost here.

But Isadora was beside herself with anger. She flailed about, waving her hands and behaving like a wild woman.

"You will choose her over me? Me? I came back for you!"

Arlo stared at his mother while Isadora grew angrier; she started crying and laughing hysterically as she attempted to grab Arlo's face. One of Isadora's hands passed through Arlo's face, but her other hand slapped his cheek. The coldness of Isadora's hand frightened Arlo, and he tried to regain control of the situation.

"Something's happening to you, Isadora."

But Isadora wasn't listening. She was furious at Arlo's desire to save his mother.

"I sacrificed my life for you, and this is how you repay me? Fuck her! It's you and me! No one else!"

Meanwhile, John and Asura slowly moved through the crowd of comatose zombies as they watched Arlo speaking to someone they couldn't see.

"Who's he talking to?" whispered John.

"His bitch," replied Asura.

Asura raised her hand, and a blue flame engulfed her arm.

"May as well take advantage of this lover's quarrel."

Suddenly, the flame on Asura's hand went out, and she stared at her palm – a Cherry Blossom petal stuck to the back of her wet hand.

"Oh no!" she yelled.

Asura grabbed John and took off running.

"We've got to get out of here! The Angels are coming!"

Arlo turned around and saw Asura and John running toward the forest.

"Stop them!" he yelled inside his mind.

Although most of the zombies were only partially through the transformation, all the zombies ran after the witch and her master. Some of the undead ran after the duo, dragging the other half of their torsos, while others chased John and Asura with heads dangling out of their chests.

Asura looked up at the sky as she ran.

"I'm not worried about those mindless zombies. We've got to get out of here before the Angels see us."

Meanwhile, Isadora continued her rage.

"You will love me as I love you!" screamed Isadora, landing a slap on Arlo's face.

But Arlo didn't care. Lightning bolts were exploding inside the cloud like fireworks. He knew they were running out of time.

Arlo spotted a few straggling zombies on the edge of the field.

"Save my mother," said Arlo inside his mind.

The zombies ran over to Claire, and one of the creatures grabbed the black vine wrapped around Arlo's mother's leg, ripped it out of her wound, and tossed it aside. The undead creature almost immediately regretted his decision; there was a rustling on the forest's edge, and the alien plant that had been sucking Claire's blood pulled its roots out of the ground and sailed through the air. It hit the zombie in the chest and wrapped its vines around its neck, choking it. As the zombie struggled to remove the vines from its neck, it made the mistake of opening its mouth; the plant shot inside the warm space, tearing off half the zombie's face while forcing its way down the monster's throat. The other zombies backed away in fear as they watched the zombie stagger about, its chest rising and falling as the plant ate his insides. Finally, the zombie fell to the ground, and its chest rose once more and fell, and the monster's entire body turned into a clear jelly. There was another rustling in the forest, and thousands of glowing worms slid to the jelly and began eating it. The other zombies quickly picked up Arlo's mother and ran into the woods.

"How dare you save her over me!" Isadora continued screaming at Arlo.

Arlo looked up – Cherry Blossom petals were raining down everywhere.

"Come on, Isadora! Let's get out of here!"

Arlo took one step and suddenly felt something massive crash into the ground. The impact was so powerful that it threw Arlo and Isadora high in the air. While he and Isadora rose above the field, Arlo saw Asura and John sailing through the air while all the zombies remained on the ground, staring at their target. The spectacle was strange to Arlo, but he knew why – it was the Angels' doing.

Arlo crashed face down in the mud so hard that he heard the bones in his face crack while Isadora tumbled head over heels and slid a few feet away. Arlo was about to get up and run when something heavy crashed into his face, knocking him to the ground. He tried to get up again and felt the excruciating pain of tree branches raking his face. Arlo closed his eyes and put his hands over his face. Suddenly, he heard the world crashing all around him; branches were snapping, screaming zombies were flying overhead, and the terrifying laughter of the Huturo, followed by their screams as something ripped them apart. Chaos was everywhere, and Arlo and Isadora couldn't get away.

"They're coming for us, Arlo!" screamed Isadora through the storm.

"Who? What is it?" yelled Arlo.

But he knew the answer to that question just as Isadora did – it was Heaven, and they were coming for them. Arlo wanted to get up and run but knew he wouldn't escape if he tried. He could only lie on the ground and wait for the madness to end.

Finally, after a few moments, everything grew silent.

"Is it over?" asked Isadora.

Arlo lifted his palm and felt his forehead – he had a massive dent in his skull. Slowly, he raised himself to his knees.

"Holy shit! What the...."

The forest that had once been there was gone; all the trees were ripped out of the ground by their roots and twisted like wire with hundreds of bodies; zombies, Huturo, vampires – all woven amongst the trees like a giant tapestry of death.

Arlo saw the carnage, and his knees grew weak.

"Mom?" he asked, looking around for signs of her body amongst the dead bodies.

"Mom?" Arlo whispered, lifting the head of a dead female zombie. "Mom, can you hear me?"

As Arlo searched nearby, Isadora started crying.

"We need to go, Arlo."

Suddenly, a lightning bolt struck one of the zombie bodies, and everything started burning. Arlo watched in horror as each of the bodies burst into flame. Arlo lost control.

"Mom!" Arlo screamed. "Mom, where are you?"

Arlo watched helplessly as the fire spread from body to body, igniting the zombies and Huturo like gasoline while mysteriously leaving the trees untouched. Isadora rose to her feet, her back covered in blood.

"I'm getting out of here," she said frantically, falling to the ground again.

"Wait," said Arlo. "How are you bleeding? Aren't you dead?"

The questions made Isadora cry harder.

"You won't let them hurt me, will you?"

Arlo stared at Isadora as the flames danced in her eyes. She resembled a child at that moment, scared and lost, begging for protection he didn't have the power to provide.

"I saved you, Arlo. Now it's your turn to save me," she cried.

For the first time, Arlo felt pity for Isadora.

"I'll take care of you, Isadora. Come on, get up."

As Arlo lifted his girlfriend off the ground, she began spilling her thoughts.

"When the Angels murdered me, I felt everything – horrible pain you can't imagine. Don't let them kill me again."

Arlo looked at the sky; the petals were pouring down on them now, and he had to wipe them from his eyes. The black cloud hovering over them now had a colossal red funnel stretching from the cloud down to the field. Although the funnel spun like a tornado, it remained stationary. Arlo traced the tube from the sky down to the ground and froze – two tall shadows stood at the base of the cloud.

"Who's that?" whispered Arlo.

Isadora looked at the shadowy figures standing at the end of the field, and her whole body shook.

"Oh, my God! I've got to get out of here!"

Isadora started climbing over the logs to escape while Arlo tried to see the faces of the men at the base of the funnel. Finally, he tried to use his powers to lift himself over the trees, but nothing happened. Arlo concentrated again, but he didn't feel the power of the dead coursing through his body. After looking back at the two shadows again, he ran after Isadora.

"Hey! Wait!"

"I can't believe it. Heaven sent Jahmel!"

Arlo climbed over the logs as Isadora hurried to get away.

"Jahmel?"

"They're Heaven's warriors. They are two of the most cold-hearted angels in existence. They're so mean Heaven only uses them to wipe names from the Scrolls of Life."

Arlo looked back and continued climbing. He remembered what the Angels did to Forneus.

"*Jah* is the one that kills the sinner. But *Mel* is the meanest. He kills everyone in the bloodline of the sinner. He loves killing whole families. Jesus, I can't believe they sent them."

"Oh, I get it. Those two are twins."

"They are always together, so the angels call them one name - *Jahmel*."

"How do you know all this?"

"As I lay on that cold floor waiting for those bastards to kill me, I listened and waited for hours. They couldn't find my name on the list and were confused. The twins fought, and I escaped when they weren't looking. That's how I came to you."

Arlo looked at Isadora suspiciously.

"How are you remembering all of this now? You couldn't even remember what you looked like when you found me."

"I don't know how, but now I can recall everything. Maybe Jahmel's presence is bringing it all back, making me human again before they kill me."

"Kill you? I doubt it. You were supposed to die a normal death. The angels killed you by accident. They came for me, not you."

"Look around, Arlo. Does this look like they're here for one soul?"

Isadora pointed to a set of small trees cluttering the road.

"There! That's our way out."

Arlo looked back and noticed the men still standing in the same spot.

"Why are they just standing there?"

"They're checking to make sure we're supposed to die. A death by eliminating someone from the Scroll of Life is not mortal. Verifications need to happen before they kill someone."

Arlo turned to look at the shadows again. Suddenly, the shadowed figures rose high in the air and began floating across the field toward Arlo and Isabella.

"They're coming, Isabella. Let's get out of here!"

Isabella was crying hysterically once more.

"I can't go back, Arlo. I just can't."

Arlo climbed over several bodies and pulled Isadora behind him.

"Less talking, more escaping," he said, climbing a large twisted tree trunk.

Once Arlo reached the top of the tree, he pulled Isadora with him. Just as he was about to jump down, Arlo spotted something a few feet away.

"Son of a bitch!" he exclaimed.

It was John! A large tree had fallen on the teenager, crushing his legs. Asura was beside him, trying to pull the tree off him. Asura stepped back from the tree and aimed her open palm at Arlo.

"Get back, you vermin!"

Arlo smiled and calmly moved closer; He knew Asura didn't have her powers. Arlo grabbed Asura by her throat and punched her in the face.

"You're a fucking coward!" barked John, struggling to free himself.

Smiling, Arlo pulled the dazed witch close and quickly placed his mouth over her nose. Arlo slurped the blood from the witch's nose until Asura's face was clean. Finally, Arlo released the woman and stared in her dazed eyes.

"Your blood tastes almost as bad as you smell, but that doesn't matter. Give me a moment to kill your master, and I'll be with you in a few seconds," Arlo whispered.

Arlo punched Asura again and tossed her limp body aside before lowering himself in front of John.

Isadora looked at the approaching angels and took off running.

"I'm sorry but I can't wait for you. I'm gone!"

Arlo watched as his girlfriend crawled over several trees.

"Whatever you do, don't look at the angels. The eyes, that's how they kill you!" she yelled before disappearing behind the fallen trees.

Arlo kneeled beside his friend.

"You caused all of this. You killed me and my father. You tortured my mother and caused all of this death. Why?"

John stopped struggling and closed his eyes.

"Everything I did was to serve Lord Balaam. I'm not afraid to die because I know he has a place for me in Hell. Do your worst."

Arlo fell on John and bit into his neck; blood sprayed everywhere. As he chewed on his friend's flesh, Arlo remembered all the pain and suffering he'd endured at his friend's hands. It wasn't John that hurt him, his name was Manuel.

Arlo raised his head between mouthfuls of flesh and spoke.

"Your name is Manuel," he growled before biting into the boy's neck again.

Arlo needed to say his name as it was. He wouldn't allow his friend the pleasure of pretending to play a part in some evil play. No, Arlo wanted Manuel to know the truth, that Manuel was the friend that betrayed Arlo for a place in Hell, a friend with whom Arlo shared years of his childhood and confessed hopes and dreams.

As Arlo filled his stomach with flesh and blood of his friend, the memories of all the time they'd spent together came rushing back. But Arlo suppressed those thoughts by eating more meat and sucking more blood. Manuel wasn't Arlo's friend anymore; he was a victim, and Arlo the murderer.

Arlo stopped eating momentarily and stared at his gasping friend; he'd almost decapitated the boy.

"I know what you're feeling now. Darkness is pulling you away from the light. But I'll give you the same gift you gave me."

Arlo thrust his face into the boy's neck and chewed through his spinal cord. He wanted Manuel to remember the pain, the scary sensation of darkness reaching out. Just as Arlo had to carry the memory of Manuel stabbing him and leaving him to die inside the cave, he wanted to give Manuel his own painful memory: the moment his friend Arlo tore his throat out and feasted on his flesh in retribution for a friendship turned sour.

Finally, Arlo rose from the ground and looked down at John – his head lay detached from his body, staring at the approaching angels. Arlo quickly scooped up John's head and turned to face Asura. The old woman was on her knees, weeping for her dead master.

"I'll eat your Master's head in peace. I want to be able to sit and enjoy his brains."

Asura glared at Arlo as he walked past. Before he disappeared, Arlo turned back to face the witch.

"I'm only allowing you to live so I can escape," said Arlo, nodding to the approaching Angels. "They'll give you everything you deserve, you bitch!"

Arlo tucked John's head under his arm and ran after Isadora.

18

Asura and the Angels

Asura remained kneeling on the ground beside her master's body, sobbing. She had cared for John since he was a child. She remembered watching over the boy when she'd allowed the demons to kill his mother and father. He'd cried so much for the first week that it was almost unbearable. He sobbed so much that Asura had to sneak out while the baby was sleeping to find his mother's body and rub the decaying corpse on her robe; the smell of his mortal mother was the only way she could calm John's weak soul.

But in time, John grew strong. He stopped leaning on the feeble ways of mortals and grew close to Asura. One of her most precious memories was teaching John how to use spells to transition to a new body. He was such a fast learner. She'd been proud when, while Asura had been out learning new spells, John had taken it upon himself to perform his first transition, independently entering a schoolmate's dreams and taking over the boy's life without her help.

Although John had taken over several souls over the years, the boy's essence remained loyal to the dark powers and fiercely protective of Asura. Now that he was gone, she wondered how she'd get along. Asura had promised Lord Balaam that she'd care for John and nurture him until she called. But now he was gone, taken by a boy Asura under-estimated. How would she explain her failure to Lord Balaam?

Suddenly, the sweet smell of strawberries interrupted Asura's thoughts, and she remembered where she was. She quickly pushed aside John's headless body and rose to her feet. Asura was about to escape when a bright violet light shone on her – it was the angels.

"What do you want?" she asked, remembering what she'd heard Isadora tell Arlo as she left.

Whatever you do, don't look at the angels. The eyes, that's how they kill you!

Asura stared at the ground without looking up until she saw two shoeless feet walk into her sight. No one spoke as the smell of strawberries flooded Asura's nostrils, sending a warm sensation coursing over her body.

"Are you here to kill me?" asked Asura.

The men remained silent as the witch stared at their feet, waiting for them to make the first move. Finally, someone spoke.

"Judgment is here," a deep voice boomed.

Asura started shaking as the voice echoed in her head.

"What do you want with me?" asked Asura, her voice trembling.

"You chose Hell over Heaven," said a second, much grittier voice.

Asura swallowed nervously and started hyperventilating.

"I... It wasn't for me! I was only..."

The voice interrupted Asura.

"There are no excuses."

Asura stared at the angels' feet, trying her best not to look up.

"There is beauty in the truth."

Asura couldn't contain herself. She quickly lifted her head and looked into the Angel's eyes. As soon as she did, her body went limp.

"So beautiful," whispered Asura.

She'd never seen something so beautiful. The Angel's eyes weren't like the eyes of a human. They were big and wide, like the eyes of a goat. There was liquid inside the enormous orbs, spinning in three tiny waterspouts, changing into strange colors she didn't know existed.

"How is this possible?" asked Asura, swaying back and forth.

Asura squinted and looked deeper into the Angel's eyes.

"Wait. I see something. It's.... It's me!"

Asura saw herself as a child, playing happily amongst a large group of children on a playground. The children were singing songs and running in a circle around Asura while Asura smiled widely. Finally, the children stopped running and hugged Asura.

"Oh my God!" exclaimed Asura, staring into the angel's eyes. "Happiness!"

Asura blinked, and the children disappeared.

"Wait. Don't go," whispered Asura, her eyes filling with tears. "Come back."

Asura wiped the tears from her eyes and looked deep into the Angel's eyes again.

"There you are. I see you," Asura whispered.

Asura saw her teenage self standing in front of a mirror. She had long black hair, lipstick, and a black dress. A thin white hand moved a brush up and down her hair as she looked away.

"I remember this," whispered Asura, staring into the eyes of the angel. "But...who's there with me?"

Finally, another face appeared in the mirror – it was her mother.

"I don't know what this obsession is with the color black," said her mom while brushing her hair. "Why don't you try wearing that nice dress Grandma gave you for your birthday?"

The teenage Asura frowned and looked away. Asura's mother stroked her daughter's hair several times before placing the brush on the dresser embracing Asura.

"You're special, Asura," said her mother. "God loves you."

Asura took in a deep breath.

"Mommy," she whispered.

Asura felt all the evil in her soul moving from her head to her chest before exiting her body through the tips of her toes.

"I-I don't want this to end. How do I..."

"Close your eyes," said both Angels.

Asura closed her eyes.

"I don't want this to end."

Suddenly, one of the angels grabbed Asura by her arms and lifted her into the air. He opened his eyes and a ray of light hit Asura in the center of her forehead. The angel let go and tilted his head back, lifting Asura into the sky. The second angel pulled a curled sickle knife out of his robe and rose. With one vicious motion, he cut Asura from the center of her forehead down her torso. Asura's body fell apart, and a blue ghostly version of herself remained floating in the air. The angel slowly stuck his hand into Asura's spirit. After fumbling around for a few seconds, he latched onto something and pulled it out. The angel lowered himself to the ground. Asura's soul remained floating in the air for a few seconds before drifting to land before the angels.

After a few moments, Asura's spirit opened her eyes. She saw the Angels standing before her and became afraid.

"Get away!" she screamed, backing away.

Asura's spirit ran past the piles of flesh that were once her human body, climbed over an enormous tree, and landed on the ground. She looked back at the angels and started yelling.

"Let me go!" she screamed.

Asura turned to run in a different direction. She crashed through shrubbery and walked through the ashes of dead Huturo, trying to escape. When she turned around, the Angels were still there, smiling.

"Get away!" she screamed.

Asura's spirit continued running until she disappeared into the night.

When Asura was gone, the Angels turned to one another and smiled.

"I rather enjoyed that, didn't you?" said Jah.

"I did. Asura needed to die. Now we can use her spirit to lead us to the other clairvoyants," replied Mel.

"Yes. After that, we'll wipe Asura's spirit from the Scrolls of Life."

Mel pulled out a tablet bearing a list of names and scratched Asura's name from his list.

"What should we do about Isadora? How much longer do you want to allow her to roam free?"

"It doesn't matter. Does it? She's already located Arlo for us."

"Allowing her to escape was a devious idea."

"It was undoubtedly wicked. Our father will not be happy. Let's hope it yields results."

"So it's settled. We'll allow Arlo and Isadora to remain free until they lead us to one of the entrances to Hell. Then we'll kill them both and wipe their names from the Scrolls of Life."

"Awesome. Let's alert the superiors. They will be pleased."